"Carly?" Puzzled, Ben reached for her again.

She didn't just pull away this time. She actually recoiled, and Ben saw fear in her eyes.

"Carly?" he repeated. What had he done?

But she was already headed down the dock, fleeing toward the cabin.

In a moment her screen door slammed shut. Ben climbed into his canoe and was halfway across the cove before he looked back at Carly's cabin. All the lights were blazing.

Something had happened to her, he thought. Something that had her terrified.

And that was just as well.

With dogged determination, he paddled toward home. It wasn't that he wished Carly Savoy pain. Quite the contrary. But whatever it was that had happened to her would keep them apart.

He hoped....

Dear Reader,

Welcome to the Silhouette **Special Edition** experience! With your search for consistently satisfying reading in mind, every month the authors and editors of Silhouette **Special Edition** aim to offer you a stimulating blend of deep emotions and high romance.

The name Silhouette **Special Edition** and the distinctive arch on the cover represent a commitment—a commitment to bring you six sensitive, substantial novels each month. In the pages of a Silhouette **Special Edition**, compelling true-to-life characters face riveting emotional issues—and come out winners. All the authors in the series strive for depth, vividness and warmth in writing these stories of living and loving in today's world.

The result, we hope, is romance you can believe in. Deeply emotional, richly romantic, infinitely rewarding—that's the Silhouette **Special Edition** experience. Come share it with us—six times a month!

From all the authors and editors of Silhouette **Special Edition**,

Best wishes,

Leslie Kazanjian,
Senior Editor

CELESTE HAMILTON
No Place To Hide

Silhouette Special Edition

Published by Silhouette Books New York

America's Publisher of Contemporary Romance

For my friend Tawnee Isbell Kirby,
who understands the need for laughter, chocolate,
long conversations about things that matter,
and an occasional afternoon at the movies

SILHOUETTE BOOKS
300 East 42nd St., New York, N.Y. 10017

ISBN: 0-373-09620-8

First Silhouette Books printing September 1990

All the characters in this book are fictitious. Any
resemblance to actual persons, living or dead, is
purely coincidental.

®: Trademark used under license and
registered in the United States Patent and
Trademark Office and in other countries.

Printed in the U.S.A.

Books by Celeste Hamilton

Silhouette Special Edition

Torn Asunder #418
Silent Partner #447
A Fine Spring Rain #503
Face Value #532
No Place To Hide #620

Silhouette Desire

*The Diamond's Sparkle #537
*Ruby Fire #549
*The Hidden Pearl #561

*Aunt Eugenia's Treasures trilogy

CELESTE HAMILTON

has been writing since she was ten years old, with the encouragement of parents who told her she could do anything she set out to do and teachers who helped her refine her talents.

The broadcast media captured her interest in high school, and she graduated from the University of Tennessee with a B.S. in Communications. From there, she began writing and producing commercials at a Chattanooga, Tennessee, radio station.

Celeste began writing romances in 1985 and now works at her craft full-time. Married to a policeman, she likes nothing better than spending time at home with him and their two much-loved cats, although she and her husband also enjoy traveling when their busy schedules permit. Wherever they go, however, "It's always nice to come home to East Tennessee—one of the most beautiful corners of the world."

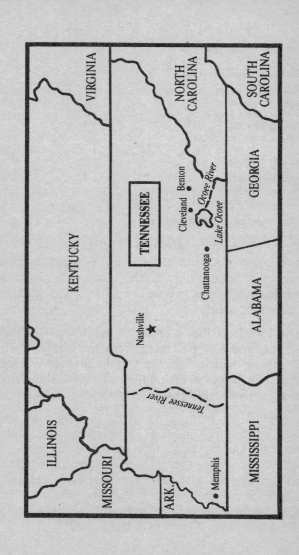

Chapter One

The quiet was astonishing.

Carly paused midway up the rickety ladder to take in the stillness of the morning. Then she realized she heard much more than silence. In the woods surrounding her father's cabin, birds cooed and chirped, calling to one another. Leaves rustled in the breeze from Lake Ocoee. A motorboat hummed in the distance. The sounds were muted, peaceful, very different from the city noises that were part of her life in New York. On this fine June morning in East Tennessee, the city seemed far away. And her only problem was a leaky roof.

Smiling, she continued her climb. The roof on the cabin's wraparound screened porch had always leaked, no matter how many times her father had patched it. During the summers Carly had spent here with him and her stepfamily, a collection of old pots and pans had stood ready to catch the drips that would develop during the slightest of showers. One summer her father had labored for two weeks, putting on a new roof. And still it had leaked. Carly could remember sleeping in the hammock on the porch and being awakened from a dream by the cold splash of rainwater in her face. When she had screamed, her father had jumped out of bed and collided in the doorway with her half sister, Diana. Soon the entire family had been in an uproar.

Poor Dad. The next morning he had climbed this very ladder yet again and cussed and fumed and fussed while his wife, Margo, had implored him to watch his language in front of the children.

Thinking of Margo made Carly laugh out loud. The way Margo had gone on about language and manners and such had belied her wonderfully adventurous nature. She had worked hard to make those summers trouble-free. If for no other reason, Carly loved Margo for the fun they'd had. Here on this lake, Carly had felt as if she belonged to a real family. How they had played. How safe they had been.

She took a deep breath of the fresh air. The tranquility of her surroundings and her happy memories filled her with a peacefulness she hadn't known in some time.

I was right to come back. Here, I'll be safe again.

Her foot was on the next rung of the ladder when a noise, sharp rather than soothing, came from near the front of the cabin. The sound came again.

Was it the snap of a twig, or the click of a gun?

Her step faltered with that last terrifying possibility. Then a man's voice cut through the morning air. Startled, she slipped and had to grab the edge of the roof to keep from falling. For a moment her feet touched nothing but air. Fear cut a path down her body as she struggled for and found a foothold. She hugged the ladder while the pounding of her heart blocked any other sound.

Except the stranger's voice.

Too frightened to understand what he was saying, she closed her eyes and prayed.

"Hey, you all right?"

When the words penetrated her panic, they were anything but threatening, yet Carly had to force herself to move. Fighting her fear, she looked down. The expression of the man gazing back at her was concerned, not menacing.

"Need some help?" he asked as he steadied the ladder.

Somehow air found its way into her lungs again. "No . . . no thanks."

The stranger rubbed a hand across the beard that covered his jaw. "I thought you were going to fall."

"You startled me." Because she was still frightened, the words were accusing.

"So I see. Sorry about that." Now his hand threaded through his tousled dark hair. "I'm Ben Jamison. Your neighbor."

So this was the cove's other occupant. When Diana had helped Carly settle in at the cabin on Sunday, she had pointed out his house but had said little about him.

"Are you a friend of the Savoys'?"

As he spoke, Carly was struck by an odd sense of familiarity. Not bothering to answer his question, she studied him closely. A beard and mustache hid most of his face, but he looked to be in his mid-thirties, about the same age as she was. Maybe they had met during one of her summers here.

He was gazing at her in a puzzled way, reminding her that she still hadn't answered his question. "Roger Savoy is my father," she explained.

Jamison nodded. "You must be the other daughter."

The description wasn't unusual. Because she had spent only vacations and some holidays with her father, she had grown used to being the "other" child. The term might have stung if she'd ever had her father to herself. But her parents had divorced when she was a baby. Her mother had remained in New York City, while her father returned to his hometown of Cleveland, Tennessee. He had married Margo, and Diana and her brother had quickly followed.

"Yes, I'm the *other* one," Carly told Jamison. "Carly Savoy. From New York."

"Well, Carly-Savoy-from-New-York." Jamison's grin was brief but pleasant, a flash of white against his dark beard. "Are you climbing that ladder for the view, or do you have a problem?"

Only then did Carly realize she was still gripping the ladder as if afraid it would fly out from under her. She relaxed a bit and wiped one perspiring palm down the side of her faded red shorts. "I've got a leak. I think last night's wind blew something loose. Rain poured in on the porch."

"We did have a gully-washer, didn't we?" Again there was that smile. It teased at the edges of Carly's memory. "Want me to come up and take a look with you?"

"I think I can manage."

"Fix many roofs?"

"No, but—"

"Come on. I'll give you a hand."

"But—"

Carly's last protest was useless since he was already climbing the ladder. She scrambled onto the roof. The distance from there to the ground seemed suddenly very far. Still feeling wobbly, she sat while she waited for him to join her.

Up close, he was taller than he had looked from her perch above him. He was tanned in the way of men who spend most of their time outdoors, and seasons of squinting into the sun had carved lines around his gray eyes. Their color was startlingly clear, and they were fringed by long lashes. Those lashes were an oddly soft touch in what was a hard male face. His eyebrows were a little too thick and straight and his nose a little too sharp for conventional handsomeness. Beneath his beard, Carly was sure his jaw was square.

He was dressed for comfort. His faded blue T-shirt sported the name of a rock band popular a decade ago. His denim cut-offs were ragged at the hem and faded to white along the seams. His legs were long. Muscular. Strong. So were his hands. One look at his hands told her he was used to working with them.

"Well, your problem's obvious," he said, pointing to a length of roofing that was hanging loose. Apparently unafraid of the height and angle of the roof, he crossed to the damaged section and pushed it back in place. "We can tack this down, but that will only be a temporary solution."

"Why is that?"

He kicked at another section with the toe of his worn leather deck shoe. "All of this looks bad."

"Do you think we need a completely new roof?"

"No. Just this part over the porch. The tin roof on the rest of the cabin was meant to last a lifetime. I told your father—"

"So you know Dad?"

His eyebrows drew together. "Didn't I say that?"

"Then you and I have met, also. Right?"

Instead of answering, he dropped to his haunches and appeared intent on the roof.

"Was it during my last summer here before college? I seem to remember—"

"No." The word was sharp. The expression in Jamison's gray eyes, a moment ago so friendly, was now ash-cold. "I don't believe we've met."

Carly was unconvinced. She almost never forgot a face, a talent that had recently served her well. *Or had it?* The question was moot, and deliberately, she pulled away from the painful memories it awakened. What had happened was in the past. She had come here to move forward. Right now, that meant finding out where she had met Ben Jamison. "I'm sure—"

"So am I," he interrupted, his tone very even and very bland. "We've never met."

"But you know my father."

"We've been neighbors for about eight years now."

It had been longer than that since she had spent any time here at the lake. From the shabby state of the cabin, she didn't think any of the family had used it much in the past year.

Jamison tugged at another loose shingle. "Roger and Margo used to spend most of the summer up here. Your sister..." He paused, as if searching for the name.

"Diana," Carly supplied.

"Right." He stood and shaded his eyes with a hand as he gazed toward the lake. "Your sister and her husband spent a lot of weekends here with their children. Your brother, too. But last summer it was pretty deserted around here."

"Dad and Margo have moved to Florida. My brother's in Colorado. As for Diana..." Carly's explanation faltered. Surely this man wasn't really so interested in her family.

He didn't seem to notice her awkward pause, and he was smiling again when he turned to her. "I can't imagine leaving a place on this lake for the heat and humidity of Florida in the summer."

Carly pushed at the strand of reddish-blond hair that had come loose from her untidy ponytail. "They intended to come back here for the summers, but Dad was so bored with retirement that he started a new business—a video-rental store, of all things."

Jamison looked surprised.

"I know," Carly said dryly. "It's not the kind of thing you'd expect from someone who hates television and professes not to have seen a movie in the past twenty years." She shrugged. "But business is booming, and now he and Margo claim they can't get away for more than a few days at a time."

"Your father never impressed me as the kind of man who could be idle for long. He was always doing something around here. Too bad he didn't get to this roof, though."

"I'll bet it hasn't been replaced in almost twenty years."

"If Roger decides to do something about it, you can tell him I'll oversee the work."

"Thanks, but I can take care of it."

"It isn't easy to get workmen to come all the way over here. It could take a few weeks."

"I'll be here all summer."

Jamison raised an eyebrow. "Getting away from the city?"

"You might say that."

For a long, silent moment, they looked at each other. Jamison's gaze was intense, giving Carly the uncomfortable sensation that he knew more than she had told him. He appeared ready to ask another question when she turned the conversation back to the roof. "Do you think this will be expensive?"

He shrugged. "Not too bad. I could do the work, if you'd like."

"I couldn't impose—"

"No imposition," he interrupted. "I like staying busy, and my place doesn't need any improvements just now."

"But surely you have other things to do."

Again he smiled. "You mean a job?"

Color stung Carly's cheeks. Perhaps the man didn't have anything else to do. Perhaps he had offered to do the repair work because he needed a job. Just because his home across the cove looked like a glass-and-stone palace from this distance didn't mean anything. "I'm sorry," she said, fumbling for a tactful way to cover her mistake. "What I meant—"

He held up a hand to stop her. "Please don't worry. I wasn't fishing for a job." Grinning, he gestured toward the spot where the cove opened into the lake. "I own a little place over that way. Sort of a combination boat rental, tackle shop and restaurant. I have some people who work for me to keep the place going. They're so good at what they do that I have plenty of free time." His grin faded. "Too much free time sometimes."

"Oh. I see." But Carly didn't really see at all. The sort of business he described couldn't possibly have bought his lakefront property or the house he had built on it. The way the man supported himself, however, was none of her business. "Of course I'll pay you for your time."

"Absolutely not," he insisted. "I'll enjoy redoing this roof. Your father and I talked about tackling it a few years back. If you're worried about my qualifications, I pretty much built my place. You could come over and inspect—"

"No, no, that won't be necessary," Carly cut in quickly. For some reason she thought Ben Jamison wasn't the sort of person who would volunteer for a job he couldn't do. She didn't know where the certainty came from, but once upon a time she was good at reading people. Once, she thought the best of people before expecting the worst. But that was some time ago. Long before snapping twigs reminded her of guns.

"Carly?"

The sound of her name made her jump, and blinking, she gazed up at Ben. Obviously he had continued talking while her mind had wandered. Funny how that happened these days. She used to be such a focused person. "I'm sorry," she said, getting to her feet. "What did you say?"

He gave her an odd look, but continued, "I said I have to drive into Cleveland early tomorrow morning. I could get the materials then, and if you'll help me, we could get this roof in shape before the weekend."

The thought of physical labor appealed to Carly. Perhaps it would help her sleep at night. "That sounds fine if you really don't mind. I have to warn you, though, I'm not too handy with a hammer and saw."

"No problem. I'm sure you'll be good at handing me things."

There was nothing patronizing about his observation, and Carly gave in to the warmth of his grin. "I believe I can do that, yes."

"And do you make good coffee?"

"Can't get started in the morning without it."

"Lemonade?"

"Straight from a can."

"Then you'll be all the help I need."

"Glad to know it, boss." She gave him a cocky salute.

Jamison's smile grew broader, and again Carly was struck by a sense of familiarity. She knew this man. Somewhere she had seen his smile. She had reacted to it. She had seen the sun glinting off his dark hair, had watched the crinkles gather around his eyes.

"I know we've met," she said.

His smile died. "Like I said—"

"But you're so familiar—"

"People are always telling me that." The comment could have been offhand, but there was an edge to his voice. Without another word he started toward the ladder.

He turned to begin his descent, and the shuttered look in his eyes sent a chill through Carly. She realized that for a few minutes she had forgotten he was a stranger, forgotten to be afraid. Maybe that indicated her wounds were beginning to heal. And maybe it only proved she was foolish. After all, they were very isolated here. Besides theirs, only one other cabin was in the cove, but it was a weekend place and situated far away. On this Tuesday morning, it was most likely abandoned. All three homes were approachable only by water. The cabin had no telephone. She was completely alone with the man who was climbing down the ladder. If he wanted . . .

Carly swallowed, fighting her panic. Sweat that had nothing to do with the warming rays of the morning sun formed beneath her loose cotton shirt. She had to get a grip on herself. Not every man she met was a threat.

"Hey," Jamison called from below, "you coming down?"

Before she could answer, the sound of a motor reached her. Turning toward the lake, she caught sight of Diana's sporty red-and-white ski boat. She had no idea what her sister was doing here on a workday morning, but Carly had never been so glad to see anyone. Ignoring Jamison, she hurried down the ladder and the steep trail to the lake. Diana was guiding the boat to a stop beside the dock when Carly reached it. Together they secured the boat, and Carly helped her sister out.

"What's wrong?" Diana surveyed her with narrowed eyes. "You look upset."

"It's nothing," Carly whispered.

Diana's voice dropped, also. "Why are you whispering?"

Carly glanced over her shoulder. Jamison was at the end of the dock, coming toward them.

The frown marring Diana's pretty features lifted as she saw him. "Don't worry. He's a neighbor." She patted Carly's arm and called a friendly greeting to Jamison. She started down the dock, swinging a plastic grocery bag jauntily at her side.

Carly could see that like most males, Jamison reacted to Diana with appreciation. The reaction was understandable. Diana was a gorgeous woman—petite but curvy, with soft blond hair and eyes of an unexpectedly clear green. She looked more seventeen than thirty in her neat white shorts and matching top. But it was her breezy manner—a trait she had inherited from Margo—that Carly had always admired and envied. She was chatting with Ben Jamison as if they were the best of friends. Carly joined them, feeling very silly about her earlier fears.

The two women really did look like sisters, Ben decided as he gazed from Diana to Carly. The resemblance hadn't occurred to him at first, but they had the same narrow face and delicate features, the same tilt to their eyes. Carly was the taller and more slender of the two. Her hair was strawberry blond, red-gold instead of moonbeam pale, and her eyes were as brown as a doe's. The eyes of a wounded deer, he thought, wondering what had caused the pain.

"Let's go up to the house and have something cool to drink," Diana suggested.

He gestured across the lake. "I really should be getting home."

"Oh, come now." Diana held up the bag she carried. "I have homemade brownies in here. Brownies made from Mom's recipe. Ben, surely you've sampled Mom's brownies."

"That I have."

"Then come on."

The thought of those brownies brought back pleasant memories as Ben followed the two women to the cabin. For the first two years he had lived on the lake, he had done little more than nod and wave to the Savoys. But when the urge to be completely alone had abated somewhat, Ben often wandered across the cove for a cup of coffee, some dessert and a visit with Roger and Margo Savoy. They were pleasant people. They didn't pry. They accepted him for what he appeared to be. He had been sorry when they hadn't shown up last summer. Yesterday, after spotting some activity at their cabin, he had hoped to find them there today.

Diana led them into the screened porch's shadowy coolness. It was pleasantly cluttered and smelled faintly musty, the same as Ben remembered from his other visits. The smell was curiously appealing, as was everything about the weathered gray cabin. No showplace, it was merely a comfortable retreat from the world.

"I see the roof's leaking again," Diana said as she started for the door to the cabin's main room.

Carly lifted a pot full of water off the table near the door and explained that Ben was going to redo the porch's roof. "Let me empty this and get us something to drink."

"No, I'll do it." Diana claimed the pot from her. "You two sit down. You're the ones who have been climbing around on the roof."

Ben took a seat at a long wooden table. Instead of joining him, Carly collected two of the half-dozen rainwater receptacles that remained scattered about on the porch.

"Let me help," he offered, and started to stand.

She waved him back into his seat. "Please, don't bother." The porch's side door squeaked as she emptied the pots outside.

"That sounds like it needs some oil."

The door banged shut, and Carly stacked the empty containers in a corner. "The roof's not the only thing around here that could use some work. I think the whole place needs a once-over."

"Especially if you're going to be here all summer."

"Yes." Moving with quick nervous energy, she disposed of two more pots of water.

Ben thought about fishing for the reason an attractive young woman would want to spend a solitary summer in this out-of-the-way spot. The same explanation probably accounted for her skittish manner and the shadows under her eyes. But he decided against pushing for details. He, of all people, knew there were plenty of reasons for wanting, *needing* to be alone.

And of course, Carly wasn't really on her own. She had her sister.

Diana appeared in the doorway, carrying a tray with a plate of brownies, a pitcher of tea, and three tall glasses of ice. "Leave the rest of those pots for me," she instructed Carly.

The slight frown of annoyance that passed over Carly's features didn't escape Ben's notice. Neither did the motherly way Diana fussed over her. Was the tea too sweet for Carly's taste? Too bitter? Were the brownies the way she liked them? Didn't she need a second one?

"Please, Diana," Carly finally said, "everything is fine. Just fine." Diana looked unconvinced, and Carly rather quickly turned to Ben. "Did you say you've had your place for eight years?"

Ben's fingers tightened around the cold glass he had raised to his lips. He nodded in answer to her question and took a long sip of tea, using the action to collect himself. Personal questions from strangers always put him on edge. This one was no exception, especially considering the way Carly had insisted she had met him before. He usually managed to turn such questions around on the asker, but Carly's earlier insistence had startled him. It had been a long time since anyone had claimed to recognize him.

"Ben lives up here year-round," Diana said before he could make a reply.

Carly looked surprised. "It must get pretty quiet in the winter. I think of this as strictly a resort area."

"It is. And it's quiet year-round. That's one of the things I like about it." Ben reached for another brownie. "I hope you're not looking for too much excitement this summer, Carly."

"Hardly."

Diana's laughter was too bright. Ben noted the tiny frown Carly directed at her.

He took the conversation in another direction. "Carly, I don't think Roger and Margo told me what you do in New York."

Her hesitation was slight but noticeable. "I was . . . uh, *am* the assistant principal of a high school. Have you always owned a tackle shop?"

Ben blinked, surprised by the way she had turned the tables on him. But he managed to recover, smiling and offering an answer that was really no answer at all. Then he asked Diana about her children, hoping Carly would take the hint and not ask about him again. He could see that she wasn't satisfied. While he chatted with her sister, she was watching him with those big, questioning brown eyes.

By remaining here, he was taking a foolish chance. In the past when people had insisted they knew him from somewhere, he had put them off and walked away. But not today. He had become so safe and so comfortable on this quiet lake that he had forgotten to keep up his guard. The mistake could cost him. It would be best to leave.

"I have to be going," he said at the first break in Diana's chatter.

"Oh, must you? Stay a while longer."

The regret in Diana's voice reminded Ben of Margo. Both mother and daughter had that coaxing Southern way of asking you to sit a few minutes more. Before he knew it, the minutes could stretch into an hour. And Carly would have a chance to continue questioning him.

He pushed away from the table, carefully not meeting her gaze. "I have a houseguest I need to check on." He noticed Diana's arched eyebrow. It was obvious she thought the guest was a woman. Ben didn't stick around to confirm or deny her suspicion. He edged toward the door, thanking them again for the snack.

"What time tomorrow?" Carly asked.

He turned around. He had forgotten his promise to repair the roof. *Damn, but that had been a stupid offer.* He cast about for an excuse, found none, and offered instead, "I'll . . . I'll . . . let you know." With a last quick nod, he pushed open the door and beat a hasty retreat down the path toward the dock.

Carly went to the door and watched him get into his canoe. His strong, even strokes carried him quickly away from the dock.

Diana cleared her throat. "That was certainly a fast departure."

"I guess he was anxious to get back to his guest."

"I'll bet she's some voluptuous redhead. He looks like the type."

Smiling, Carly turned back to her sister. "Really? How can you tell?"

"He's one of those earthy guys. You know, the back-to-nature sort. They usually go for full-figured women. I think it's the solidity that reassures them. It keeps them warm when the camp fire dies, and the hair is easy to spot when you're lost in the woods."

Carly chuckled. "Diana, you never cease to amaze me with these little gems you come up with."

The expression in her sister's green eyes softened. "Well, I'll come up with lots more if it'll keep you laughing."

Crossing her arms, Carly leaned against the door-jamb and regarded her sister with dismay. "Diana, I'm okay. You need to stop worrying about me."

"Fat chance of that after the way you came running to meet me at the boat."

Carly bit her lip. "I'm sorry about that." She explained how Ben had surprised her.

"Who did you think he was?" Diana's eyes grew wide. "Are you expecting them to send someone after you?"

"No, but I just . . . I don't know." Carly turned her gaze once more to the placid blue-green waters of the cove. How could she explain the terror that so often rose inside her without the least provocation?

"I know I don't understand," Diana said softly.

"And I hope you never do." Emotion made Carly's voice husky. She clenched her fists, trying not to imagine sweet, open Diana being brutalized.

"Do you want to talk about it?"

Carly shook her head. Talking about that cold December night that had forever altered her life was the last thing she wanted to do. In the eighteen months since, she had gone over the details so many times. The way they had surprised her. The anger in their voices. The scar on the hand that had held the gun. The horror of what they had done next. She didn't have to remember any longer. She had come here to forget.

Diana's hand on her shoulder was feather-light. Carly was relieved that she didn't flinch away from the touch. For such a long time after the attack, she couldn't bear to have anyone touch her. Now she allowed her sister to slip an arm around her waist. She drew on Diana's calm.

"I don't want you up here all alone."

The argument was the same one the sisters had been having since the night the month before when Carly had called to say she wanted to spend the summer alone at the cabin. Now she shrugged away from Diana, returned to the table and poured herself another glass of tea. "We've already been through this."

"But you were terrified when I got here."

"I'm going to get everything under control."

Diana sniffed. "By hiding away from the world? You can't learn to deal with what you avoid."

"That's a matter of opinion."

"Oh, for heaven's sake." Diana placed her hands on her hips. "You always have been the most stubborn person."

Good-naturedly Carly retorted, "And you, of course, are so agreeable."

A smile edged Diana's frown away. "Okay, so we're both stubborn. It's a Savoy trait. Our dear father and brother are just as bullheaded. I guess I'll spend this whole summer trying to get you to stay in town with me and the kids—"

"And I'll keep telling you to butt out."

"You're so sweet." Diana sat and reached for another brownie. "So, what are we going to do today?"

"We? Are you staying the day?"

"I came all the way up here. I might as well stay."

"Which brings up an interesting subject," Carly drawled. "It's not that I'm not glad to see you, but why are you here? You've been here an hour already, so it can't be your lunch break, and the thirty-minute drive from Cleveland is a little far to come for lunch, anyway, isn't it?"

Avoiding Carly's eyes, Diana crumbled her brownie. "I just didn't feel like working."

Relieved to have the conversation shift from her own problems to Diana's, Carly warned, "You're going to be fired, Diana. And just this Sunday you told me you had to keep this job."

"Would you want to spend your life typing and answering the phone at an insurance office?"

"Who says you'll be there for life?"

"Every day in that office is a lifetime." Diana dropped her chin into her cupped hand. "Why didn't I finish college?"

It was an old question. Carly gave the expected response. "You wanted to get married, remember?"

"But why didn't someone make me learn how to do something?"

"You can do lots of things."

"Oh sure, I make a mean clam dip, and I'm an expert on the application of eye makeup. Neither of those were good enough to hold Jim's interest. And neither will earn me a decent salary..." Diana paused, drawing a trembling breath. Tears gathered in her eyes.

Perhaps because she had shed so many tears of her own in the past year, Carly couldn't stand to see Diana cry. She knew from personal experience how painful divorce could be. Diana's had been all the more so because it had taken her by surprise. With no warning, Diana's husband had walked out on her and their two sons late last year. She had gone from a comfortable suburban life with a man she still loved to the challenge of earning a living for the first time in her life. The adjustment had been difficult. There were times when Carly didn't think her sister was adjusting well at all.

But Diana didn't give in to her tears this time. She wiped her eyes and gave Carly a weak smile. "You and I are quite a pair, aren't we?"

Sadly Carly had to agree. "These haven't exactly been banner years for the Savoy women."

Diana hopped up. "Well, I for one am tired of all this gloom and doom. Let's go for a swim. Who knows? Maybe the hunk across the lake will forget his houseguest and join us."

"Ben Jamison?"

"Are there any other hunks over there?"

"You think he's a hunk?"

"Of course. Don't you?"

It had been quite a while since Carly had thought about any man in terms of his attractiveness. But she could see that most normal women would find Ben Jamison appealing. She glanced across the lake, remembering the way he had looked with the sun in his hair and that smile on his face. She didn't realize she was smiling until Diana broke into her thoughts.

"My, my, maybe it really is a good thing that you've decided to spend the summer up here. Perhaps Ben's houseguest won't be staying long."

Carly sent her sister a sharp glance. "Please don't start getting ideas about me and Ben Jamison."

But Diana's expression was defiant. "I just can't believe that part of you is going to be buried forever, Carly."

"Well, I hope you're right. I never planned on being a nun." Standing, Carly began to transfer empty glasses from the table to the tray. "But I think the best I can manage right now is friendship with a man." She shrugged. "And who knows, maybe Ben will become a friend."

"Men and women don't become friends," Diana said in a dry tone.

With a groan, Carly picked up the loaded tray, only half listening to her sister's comments about male-female dynamics. Something told her that by the end of the day she was going to wish Diana hadn't played hooky from work.

* * *

Carly and her sister were swimming. From his perch on the deck that jutted out from his living room, Ben could see them in the water near their dock. Occasionally their shouts and laughter floated across the cove. The sounds only served to remind him of how alone he had felt lately.

Alone. Funny how the word had a different ring to it these days. Eight years ago he had been searching for a place he could be by himself. This corner of southeastern Tennessee had fit his specifications exactly. He had built his home and started his small business. For eight years he had measured time by the rise and fall of the water level, by the change in foliage on the surrounding mountains. His life, once as chaotic as a hurricane, was calm. Peaceful. Wasn't that what he had wanted?

He avoided the question by reaching for the glass of lemonade balanced on the railing beside him. Tart and cold, the drink slipped down his dry throat. With the back of his hand, he brushed a trickle of sweat from the side of his face. His eyes never left his neighbor's dock. How long had they been out in the midday sun? Two hours? Three? He thought of Carly's too-pale skin. She'd be badly burned if she didn't watch it.

But of course, that was no concern of his.

Damn. He should have left the moment she said he looked familiar. But no. Instead he had offered to come back. Where was his head? Now he needed an excuse not to help with her roof. He could just not show up, but that didn't seem fair. He was her parents' friend.

He frowned at the description. To say he was Roger and Margo Savoy's friend was stretching the relationship. He had only one friend, really. Not even the pair of aging hippies who ran his business could be classified as more than acquaintances.

From behind him came the whisper of a glass door sliding open and closed. Ben didn't move as his one and only friend crossed the deck. He said nothing as the man braced his arms on the railing and sighed. For a long moment, there was silence.

Then his friend spoke, his voice deep and rich, his tone thoughtful. "Would it be so bad?"

Ben turned to gaze at the familiar, distinctly Italian features.

Stefan cocked his head toward the opposite shore. "Would it be so bad if she realized who you are?"

Chapter Two

Moonlight shimmered on the waters of the cove and then was gone. With his paddle poised over the water, Ben glanced up. The moon had ducked behind a cloud. Rain, he decided. The night smelled like rain. Come morning Carly would have more water leaking through her roof. Realizing the direction his thoughts had taken, he cursed and stroked his paddle hard through the water. The canoe surged forward, away from his home and the cabin across the way.

Where the cove joined the lake, he stopped paddling and allowed the boat to drift. *Drifting.* Stefan had said Ben was drifting through life. But then, Stefan had had plenty to say this afternoon. Ben had come to regret telling his friend about the way Carly had almost recognized him. The information was the opening Stefan needed to begin his usual tirade about what Ben was doing with his life. Ben had been in retreat from the older man's badgering when Stefan had trapped him on the deck this afternoon.

"Would it be so bad if she recognized you?" Stefan had repeated when Ben didn't answer him.

"We've been through this before. I don't want to be recognized."

"But why? What do you think would happen?"

Ben shrugged, turning away from the older man's shrewd brown eyes. Stefan's hair might have turned completely white in the past year, but he was as insightful as ever.

"Do you think you're still so hot that reporters would swarm over here?"

"Of course not. I never thought I was that hot. Not really."

Stefan brushed the comment aside with a dramatic sweep of his hand. "Who are you trying to fool, Ben? This is me. Stefan Scolari. I know you, remember? I know just how great you thought you were. That ego of yours was one of your problems."

"My ego took a pretty good thrashing."

"Down but not out. If you decided to come back—"

"Stefan, I don't want this. I don't need it." Ben slipped from his perch on the railing and moved to the other end of the deck.

Several moments went by before Stefan said, "You'll always regret it, you know."

Stoically gazing at the mountains that rose behind his house, Ben sighed. "You're right. I'll always have plenty of regrets."

"I mean you'll regret giving it all up."

"You know why I gave it up. Do you think I'd even be alive if I hadn't?"

"Yes," Stefan replied quietly. "Yes, I do. You were strong enough to survive in the end."

Ben turned to him again, shaking his head. "You're wrong. If I hadn't walked away, I'd be dead right now. And God only knows who else I would have taken to the grave with me."

Stefan cursed in Italian.

Grinning, Ben wagged a finger in his direction. "Now, now. Remember, Mother always insisted you do us the courtesy of cursing in English."

"Your mother, God rest her soul, was a beautiful but completely illogical woman. I've never quite understood how she managed to raise you."

Ben sobered. "If you'll recall, I didn't use to be such a credit to her."

"She didn't feel that way."

"Maybe she should have."

Pushing both hands through his hair in a disgusted gesture, Stefan cursed again. "You know your problem, Ben? The world is still black and white to you. Right. Wrong. Bad. Good. There's no middle ground."

"I have to think of it that way. The gray area is where I always get lost."

"Lost?" Stefan shoved both hands into the pockets of his loose cotton shorts. "Don't you think you're lost now? Living here. Turning your back on the life you were meant for."

"But I like it here," Ben retorted mildly. "I'm happy."

Stefan snorted. "No, you're not. You're just drifting. You've been drifting since you and Angela divorced."

The name sent a dull pang through Ben. Even now, hours after their conversation ended, he was still reacting to Stefan's mention of his ex-wife. Thoughts of Angela had sent him out of the house and into his canoe in hopes that exercise would relax him. But his body was tense as he pulled his paddle through the water again. Silently the canoe skimmed along. By memory Ben navigated the calm waters, following the contour of the shore opposite his own property.

Stefan had been right about a few things this afternoon. Grudgingly Ben admitted to himself what he would never have admitted to his friend. To him the world *was* black and white. Angela had been good. He had been bad. And in the end the bad had crushed the good. Stefan could argue and bluster all he wanted, but that was one point that couldn't be altered. And because of that, Ben would never return to his old life. He lived with his failures on a daily basis, but at least here on this peaceful lake he was in no danger of being seduced by the temptations that had destroyed Angela and almost taken him.

There were times—sleepless nights mainly—when Ben replayed the events that had led him to his current situation. As the years slipped past, his old life had begun to seem like a dream. Or perhaps *nightmare* was the more appropriate term. No, he decided, that wasn't fair. Despite the lack of a father, his childhood had been a good one. He'd had every reason to have a good life. His mother had worked hard to make him happy and secure. Maybe their life hadn't been conventional, but it had been full of love.

Thoughts of his mother at last relaxed the tension that had gripped his body. Ben wondered if she would agree with Stefan that he was wasting his life. Certainly she wouldn't have been happy to live here. For all her seeming naïveté Leslie Kyle had favored bright lights over moonbeams. She liked city noises, city comforts. When others had complained about the Los Angeles smog, she would take a deep breath and smile, saying it beat the smell of Nebraska cornfields in her book.

Ben smiled, trying to imagine his mother visiting here on the lake. Like Stefan, she probably could have endured it for a week or two every year. She and Stefan would have sat on the deck and bickered in their usual, good-natured way, and Ben could have served as referee, just as he'd always done. He supposed they would look like any other family. Over the years, strangers, seeing the three of them together, had automatically assumed they were a family. And in an odd sort of way, they had been a unit—his beautiful single mother, debonair Stefan, and himself.

When he was very young, Ben used to fantasize that Stefan really was his father. Later he came to understand that it didn't matter. Stefan had cared for him. Still did. Why else would the man continue to come here and beg Ben to return to the fold? No week passed without some word from Stefan. The bond between them hadn't died with Ben's mother.

God, the times the three of them had shared. The very best of times. Allowing his canoe to drift again, Ben's mind skipped from memory to memory, until his thoughts carried him to the dark days. The days he wished he could forget.

The past. Somehow he could never quite put it aside. It was like an exotic snake—beautifully colored, mesmerizing and oh-so-deadly. If it got too close, it poisoned his peace of mind.

The scrape of a rock beneath the canoe made Ben realize he had drifted near the shore. Using his paddle, he pushed away and glanced around. Though clouds had again covered the moon, he could see the Savoys' dock ahead. His aimless wandering had brought him right back to his problem. How was he going to avoid Carly Savoy?

Silently his paddle sliced through the water, carrying him closer to her dock. The lights glowed in her cabin. The sight was somehow comforting. Except for weekends, the cove was usually dark and silent and uninhabited. On nights such as this, when the air was still and quiet in expectation of a storm, he often felt as if he were the only person left alive in the world. This summer would be different. Every night he would be able to see the lights from Carly's house. Ben didn't know why, but as he drew alongside the Savoys' small boathouse, the thought made him laugh out loud.

And then someone screamed.

Carly. The memory of her wide, frightened brown eyes flashed in Ben's head. Then there was a crash on the dock and he sprang into action.

Later, he was never sure how he got so quickly to the Savoys' dock. One minute he was in the canoe, and the next he was scrambling across the rough-hewn planks toward the covered boathouse where he thought the scream had come from. The night was dark and the dock unfamiliar. He tripped over something and fell to his knees just as the moon flitted from behind a cloud. Looking up he saw Carly flattened against the wall beside the boathouse.

"You!" she gasped. "What the hell are you doing?"

He struggled to his feet, rubbing a knee. "What am I doing? What are you doing? What happened?"

"I heard . . . I mean . . ." She pressed a hand to her mouth. "I was sitting here, and someone laughed—"

"That was me."

"You? But I thought . . ."

"What?" Ben prompted, stepping closer. "What did you think?"

She shook her head. Moonlight was streaming across the dock, bright enough that he could pick out the red-gold highlights in her hair. Her eyes looked bigger and more frightened than ever. Ben could see that she was shaking.

"You're terrified." He reached out to take her arm, but she shrugged away.

"No, I'm okay," Carly said, drawing a deep breath as she turned toward the boathouse. "There's a light around here somewhere." She felt along the wall of the boathouse until she found a switch. Light bloomed from the small fixture beside the door. "Now, that's better."

"The light is. Are you?"

Still not looking at him, Carly nodded. She pointed toward the other side of the dock. "What about your canoe? Won't it drift away?"

While he went to take care of his boat, Carly berated herself. The man must think her a fool. Twice in one day she had dissolved into a mass of nerves in front of him. But of course that wouldn't have happened if he hadn't surprised her. Annoyance with him replaced her fear as he crossed the dock. "What are you doing sneaking around here, anyway?"

He stopped in his tracks, blinking. "Sneaking?"

"That's right. This makes the second time today you've snuck up on me."

"What are you talking about? I have no reason to sneak up on you." Scowling, he placed both hands on his hips.

"Then what are you doing over here at this time of the night?"

"Canoeing."

"In the dark?"

"Is there some reason I shouldn't?"

Carly swallowed. There was no reason, of course. None, aside from the fact that she was so ridiculously easy to startle. And that wasn't his fault.

His scowl disappeared, replaced by concern. "Listen, I didn't mean to frighten you. Not tonight or earlier today. I'm sorry." Hand outstretched, he stepped toward her again.

She retreated and reached for the lawn chair he had tripped over. "I guess I'm sorry, too. I didn't mean to scream like that. But you laughed—"

"No one's ever told me it was such a terrifying sound."

Glancing up, she caught his smile. Continuing to be afraid of a man with a smile so genuine was ridiculous. She gathered the last of her scattered nerves and set the chair to rights. "I just wasn't expecting to hear someone laugh. It's late, and I thought I was alone."

"I didn't expect anyone to be sitting out here in the dark, either. When I heard you scream, I didn't know what to think."

"I'm...uh...I guess I'm a little nervous about being alone in a strange place."

"Strange? But didn't Diana say this afternoon that you used to spend every summer here?"

"Yes, but it's been years and years. And I..." Carly gazed heavenward. She wasn't sure how to explain the reason she found herself jumping at shadows. "It's just so different from being in the city," she provided finally.

"Missing it already?"

Her laugh was short. "Missing it? No. Not at all."

"Yeah." He sucked in his breath. "Who could miss the city on a night like this?"

"That's why I was down here—because it is such a nice night." *And it's been so long since I've been able to enjoy a night,* Carly added to herself.

"It's going to storm."

Her gaze followed his to the sky. "It looks to me as if the clouds are moving out of the way."

"Believe me, I know the signs, and we're in for a good one later tonight."

"Great. Another porch flood."

"But not for long. We'll get the roof fixed." The minute he uttered the words Ben wanted to call them back. He was trying to avoid this woman, not become more entrenched. How was it she managed to make him forget that?

"Would you like to sit down for a few minutes?"

He almost refused. A glance at her face changed his mind. She was nervous and alone. She seemed very fragile, in need of his protection. It had been a long time since Ben had felt someone needed his protection, needed anything from him. So instead of following the practical dictates of his head, he took the seat she offered. He could at least stay until the frightened look in her eyes was gone.

She took the aluminum lawn chair opposite his. "I really am sorry. I hope you didn't hurt yourself when you tripped. I knocked over the chair myself when I heard you laugh."

His left knee was aching, but it was nothing serious. "A bruise or two is to be expected when rescuing a damsel in distress."

He had hoped to make her smile. Instead, she twisted her hands together in her lap. "I feel very foolish."

He thought about reaching out and patting her arm, but then changed his mind. Something told him she'd jump right out of her seat if he touched her. "Let's just forget it. And from now on, I'll try to remember I'm not alone in the cove anymore. In return, you can try to keep from screaming. The sound took a few years off my life." He rubbed his beard. "I wouldn't be surprised if this were white."

The tiniest of grins at last curved her lips. *Her pink, sweetly shaped lips.* Ben decided a man could forget all honorable intentions if he gazed too long at Carly's mouth. The thought took him by surprise and, frowning, he quickly glanced away. Being attracted to this woman was the last thing he wanted. Not that there was any danger of letting those feelings get out of control, but still . . .

Deliberately turning from the direction his thoughts were taking him, he searched for a safe, impersonal topic. "Have you got your father's boat here in the boathouse?"

Carly nodded. "It's old, and Diana worries about it. But then, Diana worries about my being up here, period."

"I sort of noticed that."

"Well, she makes no effort to hide her feelings."

"And she drives you crazy," he observed dryly, swatting at a mosquito.

Genuine laughter, the first Ben thought he had heard from Carly, tumbled out. "I guess in that respect little sisters never change." Beginning to relax at last, she shifted in her chair, drawing one leg up under her.

"You and Diana seem to get along pretty well, though," he said, forgetting that he wanted to keep the conversation impersonal.

"I guess we do. I'm sure I drive her nuts sometimes, too." Absentmindedly, she twirled a tendril of hair that had escaped from her untidy ponytail. Ben followed the movement of her hand and wondered if her hair would feel as fine and soft as it looked. She released the tendril, and it brushed against her shoulder. She was sunburned there, just as he had thought she would be. The skin was rosy against her white knit top. Rosy, just like her cheeks.

"Ben?"

With a start he realized he had been staring at rather than listening to Carly. She was regarding him with a wary expression. He managed a smile. "I'm sorry. I was out of it there for a minute. What did you say?"

"I asked if you have a family."

The question should have made him uncomfortable. He should have immediately begun thinking of evasions, but instead he found himself wanting to give her a truthful answer. For the first time in a long while, Ben felt like sharing something of himself—his true self—with someone other than Stefan. Wondering if he was making a mistake, he followed his impulse. "Well, I don't have a brother or a sister. There was only my mother. She's been gone nearly twelve years."

"I'm sorry." The comment might have sounded perfunctory, but Ben felt the underlying sincerity.

He braced himself, expecting an onslaught of personal questions about why he didn't mention a father. But Carly didn't press for the details he had usually found too painful to share. Softly she said, "Losing a parent is probably never easy, but being an only child makes it worse, I think."

"Maybe."

"Of course, I have four parents, and that isn't easy, either."

"Four?"

"Dad and Margo. My mother and her husband."

"Don't you like your stepfather?"

Carly shrugged. "He and Mother didn't marry until I was in high school. That's probably not the best time for a girl to gain a new parent. I was in my rebellious stage. He didn't know quite what to make of me."

"What about now?"

"He still doesn't know what to make of me. We sort of glare at each other across the dinner table on holidays and occasional Sundays."

Chuckling, Ben stretched his legs out in front of him. "The picture I'm getting isn't quite like a Norman Rockwell painting."

"Not quite," Carly agreed, and let her laughter blend comfortably with his. Considering how only a short while ago she had been terrified, she was amazed at how relaxed she now felt with this man. Maybe it was because he still reminded her of someone she had once known. Surely who that someone was would come to her sooner or later. "You're not from around here, are you?" she asked.

She had noticed this morning how reluctant he was to talk about himself, so as she expected, he answered with another question. "Why wouldn't you think I'm a native?"

"No accent, for one thing."

"But not everyone from around here has a broad Southern drawl."

"Most of them do."

"Well, you don't sound like a typical New Yorker, either."

She bristled slightly. "Oh, and what's typical?"

He laughed. "Something tells me we could get into quite a regional argument if we keep this up."

A very neat way of avoiding any questions, Carly decided. But perhaps that was just as well. He seemed to be a nice-enough fellow. Diana had said their parents had liked him. If he had secrets, well, didn't everyone?

"It's lightning," he said.

Carly followed his gaze. Lightning was indeed dancing over the mountains in the distance. Thunder, faint but still noticeable, rolled. The wind was picking up, too. Clouds had again covered the moon. "I guess you were right about the storm," she said, shivering a little.

His eyebrows drew together in a frown. "Are you going to be all right over here?"

She sat up straighter. "Of course. It stormed last night, and I was fine."

"But—"

"I'll be okay," she insisted in a soft but firm voice. "But you won't if you're caught out on the water."

"I suppose you're right." He stifled a yawn and stretched, lifting his arms over his head. "I should get home."

Carly tried her best not to notice the firm muscles revealed by his sleeveless shirt. She told herself she wouldn't have noticed at all if Diana hadn't made such a point of discussing his physical attributes this morning. Those attributes were, however, hard to ignore. They proved Diana had been right. Ben Jamison was a hunk. He was pleasant, too. The combination made him an extremely attractive man. To her surprise, Carly felt good about admitting that to herself. She felt normal. And normalcy was all she wanted.

He stood, and her gaze went to the length of tanned leg revealed by his ragged cut-offs. Then, guiltily, she looked away and got up, also. "I'll see you tomorrow, I hope." To her ears she sounded a little too eager. "I mean," she amended, striving for a light note, "if you still want to work on the roof. I know you have a houseguest and everything."

Ben hesitated a long moment. It wasn't until he smiled that Carly realized she was holding her breath. "I'll see you some time tomorrow," he agreed. Rather pointedly, or so Carly thought, there was no mention of his guest.

Feeling stiff and awkward, she shifted from foot to foot. Ben started toward his canoe, and she turned to follow. Perhaps his leg brushed hers or maybe there was a loose plank in that particular section of the dock. Whatever the case, Ben stumbled into Carly. For half a heartbeat, she held his weight against her own. Then he recovered his balance. But he didn't pull away. The dynamics changed so that he was holding her.

He was warm, solid, male. For one small but charged moment, Carly allowed herself to enjoy the feel of his body against her own. She knew Ben felt what passed between them, too. The knowledge was in his shadowed gaze, in the hands that tightened around her waist. God, it had been so long since she had been held.

But as suddenly as the moment was born, it died, shattered by the memories of other hands, other touches. The terror, as always, engulfed Carly. Gasping, she wrenched away from the arms that held her.

"Carly?" Puzzled, Ben reached for her again.

She didn't just pull away this time. She actually recoiled, and Ben saw the fear in her eyes again.

"Carly?" he repeated. *What had he done?*

She was already headed down the dock, toward the path to the cabin. "Good night," was all she took the time to call over her shoulder.

In a moment her screened-porch door slammed shut, the sound underscored by a peal of thunder. Ben took the time to shut off the dock's light before climbing into his canoe. He was halfway across the cove when he looked back at Carly's cabin. All the lights were still blazing.

Something had happened to her, he thought. Something that still had her terrified.

And that was just as well.

With dogged determination, he paddled toward home. It wasn't that he wished Carly Savoy pain. Quite the contrary. But whatever it was that had happened to her would keep them apart.

He hoped.

With a glass of wine in one hand and a cigar in the other, Stefan was waiting for Ben on the lighted deck. "I was beginning to worry," he chided. "The storm is coming closer."

"Sorry. I was sort of delayed."

The older man's smile was a slice of white in his tanned face. "And did the woman across the lake recognize you?"

"How do you know that's where I've been?"

"Haven't I always known where you could be found?"

Ben nodded. Back in the old days, Stefan had always known which gutter to pull him out of.

"You haven't answered my question."

"No," Ben said. "She didn't recognize me."

"A pity."

To his immense surprise, Ben found himself agreeing. Maybe that meant Stefan was right. Maybe he had been alone in his secluded little cove for too long.

The storm hit at midnight. Carly had hoped to be asleep by then. After swimming most of the day, she was physically tired, but sleep still wouldn't come. She was keyed up, full of the nervous energy that usually kept her awake. Thunder and lightning suited her mood all too well.

Nights were always difficult. Tonight was worse than usual, however, because of her encounter with Ben Jamison. Why had he frightened her so? Why did she still feel like someone sitting in the path of a tornado? She couldn't run from the fury. She couldn't hide. Not even in this quiet lakeside retreat.

A stereotypical rape victim. Carly grimaced as she silently repeated those words. Dammit, she had never been a stereotype before. She had lived by her own set of rules. Even right after the attack, she had put her head up and marched straight back into life. She had put on a grand charade for everyone. Until six months ago. Until the trial was over. Until a black hole of fear had seemed ready to swallow her at every turn.

The psychologists had a name for it. Post-traumatic stress. Carly hadn't wanted to admit to any weakness. But she had. Then she had tried to work through it. That's what this summer was about. A change of scenery. A peaceful vacation from the gangs and the drugs and the problems that crawled through the inner-city school where she worked. Far from the place where she had been attacked. Perhaps two days wasn't adequate time in which to judge, but the interlude was proving anything but idyllic.

And all because of the man across the lake.

That problem was probably solved now. After tonight he would be keeping his distance, and she couldn't blame him. A crazy woman who screams at the sound of laughter and runs from the most innocent of touches wasn't anyone's idea of an interesting companion.

Tonight had one positive side, though. Carly had at long last been able to feel something for a man again. Yes, the fear had caught up with her, but she had made a start. Someday, maybe, she would conquer the terror.

Lightning flashed, and Carly glanced at her watch. Half-past midnight, and still she sat here, wide awake. The pills her doctor had prescribed were on the counter that separated the tiny kitchen from the rest of the cabin. Briefly she considered them, but then turned away. She didn't want to rely on artificial escape. She picked up a book, then a magazine. The rhythm of the rain on the tin roof might have lulled her to sleep. Unfortunately, the splash of water in the pans on the porch interfered with the harmony. Giving up, she settled on her normal cure-all. She cleaned.

In the past long months, she had often considered hiring herself out nightly as a cleaning person. Every inch of her once-untidy apartment had been disinfected. Her closets and cupboards were so organized she had been forced into tearing them apart and putting them back together—just to have something to do at night. But the cabin represented a fresh challenge.

Of course, the main floor didn't need much tidying, since she had attacked it last night. It was one room, basically. Two lumpy sofas and a couple of rockers sat in front of the big stone fireplace that divided the back wall. The alcove on one side of the fireplace contained the kitchen. In the other was a small bathroom. The front corner was occupied by her bed. In the other was the staircase to the two bedrooms on the top floor. Carly had only glanced in those rooms since arriving. Now, armed with broom and dust cloth, she climbed the stairs.

The tiny front room was the one she and Diana had shared when not sleeping on the porch during the summer. Little had changed since the days they had giggled and shared secrets here. The two cots were stripped bare, and the bold purple paint on the walls had faded a bit. White curtains had replaced the orange ones they had hung on the windows and across the closet doorway. Orange and purple. Chuckling, Carly turned slowly in the center of the room. Why in heaven's name had that color combination been so appealing at age sixteen? Surely Margo had regretted allowing them control of the decorating scheme. After the roof was fixed, Carly decided she would paint this room.

"A nice bright yellow," she murmured. She could starch the curtains, too. The result would be a pleasant rainy-day retreat for Diana's two boys when they visited. "Or maybe I'll buy new curtains," she said when the cloth covering the closet opening almost disintegrated at her touch. "Doesn't anybody stay up here anymore?" she murmured aloud.

Apparently not. The closet was full of boxes and assorted paraphernalia. Some dirty sneakers. A flattened volleyball. A broken water ski and two neat stacks of magazines.

"God, Margo *would* keep these." Carly decided her entire four-year collection of teen magazines was in this closet. Unable to spend three months without the pictures of her teenybopper idols, she had hauled them back and forth between New York and Tennessee every summer, much to her father's chagrin. Each month she had collected five or six new ones. Diana had done the same. At one time this room had been plastered with four-color photographs. Then Carly had bloomed at long last and begun attracting boys during her sixteenth summer here on the lake. Diana, two years younger but always precocious, had done the same. The fantasy figures had been forgotten in favor of the real thing. Summer nights on the moonlit lake had provided the backdrop for her first tastes of romance.

The pleasant memories flooded back as Carly opened a magazine on the top of the stack. She and Diana had had a serious discussion about whether Carly was betraying her favorite star by kissing some boy they had met over at the public beach on the other side of the lake. What was that boy's name? Jimmy something. And who was the idol? So much for swearing never to forget him.

Laughing, Carly picked up an armload of magazines and settled on the cot. Dust rose in a cloud as the mattress gave under her weight. Already absorbed in her trip to the past, she barely noticed.

She awoke on the cot the next morning. Blinking at the sun that poured through the window, she sat up and glanced at her watch. It was well after nine, the latest she had slept in months. Smiling, feeling content, she stretched. The glow followed her to the shower. It lingered as she made coffee. It only intensified when she went out onto the porch and saw Ben Jamison climbing the steep path from the lake.

In a white tank top and the usual cut-offs, toting a toolbox, he looked hot and tired. Sweat had never appealed much to Carly. Until now. Somehow, on Ben Jamison, perspiration took on a new dimension. Perhaps it was the way it shimmered on the sleek muscles of his arms. Or maybe it was the faded bandanna he had tied around his sweat-dampened hair that did the trick. For whatever reason, he took her breath away. And the last thing she felt like doing was running away.

Grunting, he swung the box of shingles to the steps and dropped the toolbox. Carly pushed open the door.

"Well," he said, grinning, "are you just going to stand there? Where's my coffee?"

Startled, she glanced down at her steaming mug.

"We did have a deal. Coffee and lemonade in exchange for a new roof. Come on, let's get this show on the road.'' He wiped a trickle of perspiration from the side of his neck and winked.

So she hadn't chased him away, after all. She returned his grin, flooded by unexpected relief. Then she scurried inside.

''I take cream, too,'' he called after her.

Feeling as giddy as she had at sixteen, Carly started another pot of coffee. Ben Jamison looked like the kind of man who wouldn't be satisfied by one or two cups. He wouldn't be satisfied by small measures of anything.

She chose to ignore the implications of that thought.

Chapter Three

Since moving to the lake, Ben had discovered the healing benefits of working with his hands. Measuring, cutting, pounding nails—they were deceptively simple tasks. In reality they demanded thought, concentration and skill. A man could lose himself in this kind of work, and when it was finished he had something real to show for his labors. Ben had worked hard many times in his life. He had earned a fortune. But money alone had never satisfied him. Being able to take pride in what he accomplished was the only goal that mattered.

The house he had fashioned of stone and wood and glass pleased him. Working at an easy pace, he had used professionals for the tricky parts of the construction and had accomplished the rest on his own by turning to how-to books and the trial-and-error method. The work had continued for years as he added a deck here, an extra room there. In between home projects, he had worked on the building that housed his business. Sometimes he thought carpentry was his true calling.

The people he had once called friends would have laughed at the importance he now placed on a well-painted wall or a door that closed without a squeak. He thought they would benefit from several hours spent earning some real sweat in the summer sun.

Carly seemed to share his respect for honest physical labor. Yesterday morning and the past two afternoons, she had crawled around her porch roof with him. As she had indicated, she was no expert with a hammer and nail, but she did follow instructions. What she lacked in skill she made up for in companionship. Not that they talked much. Quite the contrary. But Carly betrayed more with a smile than most of the phonies in Ben's old life had conveyed in an entire conversation.

He liked Carly's smile. It started in the depths of her brown eyes and spread downward till it curved her soft lips and tilted the tip of her pert little nose. Ben knew without a doubt that he could sit and look at her smile all day. He didn't stop to wonder why a relative stranger's smile should mean so much. He just accepted her smiles. Reveled in them.

Then there was her laugh. Given the chance, he was sure he could wax eloquent about the sound of it.

Perhaps it was because she didn't laugh all the time. But when she did, he got the feeling she meant it, felt it, all the way to her toes.

To his surprise she cursed with the same gusto. During that first morning of work, when she had smashed her fingers more times than she had hit the nail, Ben had been amazed by some of the words that had come out of her pretty mouth.

"My father taught me," she had explained when he looked askance at a particularly colorful expletive. "He said you shouldn't curse much, but when you did you should do it well."

It was just the perverse sort of advice Ben could imagine Roger Savoy giving. Today, as Ben squinted into the hot midafternoon sun, he thought about indulging in some foul language of his own. It was only June, and already the temperature was climbing to the nineties on a regular basis. For days the humidity had been building.

He doffed his baseball cap, wondering if Carly wanted to knock off for the day. If they pushed it, they could finish this afternoon. But that would mean he would have no excuse to return tomorrow. In all honesty Ben knew he could have finished yesterday. Deliberately he had taken his time. The thought of a day without Carly's smile left him with a hollow feeling.

Other than the pounding of a hammer, it had been quiet this afternoon on her side of the roof. He was just about to ask her how it was going when she let out a yell.

Chuckling, Ben tugged the baseball hat back on. "What did you do this time?"

"I dropped the...uh...the hammer over the side again."

He scrambled around the corner and grinned at her. "What kind of hammer did you say it was?"

Carly was near the front edge of the roof, peering down at the ground. "My good conscience didn't allow me to say what kind of hammer. I've been trying to clean up my mouth today."

"Why?"

"Because Margo would die if she heard me."

"But Margo isn't here."

"Call me crazy, but the habits of a lifetime die hard." Sitting back on her haunches, Carly jerked a thumb toward the ladder. "At any minute I expect to see her climbing up here with a bar of soap in her hand."

The image didn't jibe with the calm, gentle woman Ben had come to know during past summers. "She washed your mouth out with soap?"

"No, but she threatened to a lot, especially when we came out with some of Dad's better expressions."

"But wasn't that his fault?"

"Of course."

"Then why didn't she wash out his mouth?"

The suggestion prompted one of Carly's belly laughs. "That's what I'd like to see," she managed between shouts of laughter. "Little bitty Margo giving it good to big ole Dad. No matter how mad she got at us, he could do no wrong."

"Some people would call that a perfect marriage."

"Well, if it was perfect, it was all Margo's doing. Dad could be a bear when he wanted to."

"I always thought kids hated their stepmothers."

Carly tsk-tsked. "Another fallacy perpetuated by outdated fairy tales."

"Ah-ha!" Ben exclaimed. "Now you sound like an educator."

"And how do educators sound?"

"Full of moral outrage and the thirst for truth and knowledge," he intoned solemnly.

She rolled her eyes heavenward. "Where do you pick up these notions, Mr. Jamison?"

"My experience with educators wasn't entirely enjoyable. Not for me or for them."

"Sounds as if you were a problem child. Probably the same sort I see in my office day after day."

He allowed his gaze to slip over her, taking in the faded, short denim overalls and blouse. Hours in the sun had given her a light tan and raised a coppery smudge of freckles across her nose. Her hair was tucked under an old straw hat. Adorable was the only way he could think to describe her. "If you had been my vice-principal," he began and then thought better of the comment.

"You'd what?" she pressed.

He rubbed his beard and decided on the truth. "I'd have made up excuses to be in your office."

As expected, her gaze faltered under his. Nervously she tugged at the brim of her hat, blocking her face from his view. "I believe you were probably what we in the education field call incorrigible."

Ben grinned, pleased that she had responded instead of changing the subject. "I guess I'm still that way."

"Most assuredly." Beneath the hat, he caught the flash of her smile.

Were they flirting? Ben wasn't sure. In recent years, male-female repartee hadn't played much of a part in his life. There had been some women, yes. Infrequent, impersonal encounters with women who shared his need for purely physical release. When that didn't feel like enough, he reminded himself it was all he deserved. No one since Angela had touched him as did this slim, rather nervous woman.

"Come on," he said, pushing to his feet.

Carly glanced up, regarding his outstretched hand with suspicion. "What do you mean?"

"Let's leave this roof to bake in the sun while we go for a swim."

"A swim," she repeated.

He stroked the air with his arms. "You know. In the water." Again he offered her his hand. "Come on, Carly. Let's cool off."

This time she allowed him to pull her to her feet without hesitation. Carly couldn't tell if Ben sensed what an effort that simple action was. He merely smiled that devilish pirate's smile of his and turned to climb off the roof. She followed. Fifteen minutes later she had changed into her suit and was headed across the dock.

If putting her hand in his had been difficult, walking across the dock in her modest one-piece was sheer torture. She was thankful he was already in the water, diving in and out like a young seal. He called a greeting and disappeared under the surface. After tossing some towels onto a lounge chair, she took a seat on the ladder built into the side of the dock. She shivered as her feet trailed through the water. Despite the sweltering weather, the water was cold. It even looked cold today, more blue than green, a reflection of the cloudless sky.

A touch on her foot brought her gaze down. Ben grinned at her. "Come in," he invited.

She pulled her foot from his grasp and stood on the ladder. "I usually take my time getting in. The water's chilly."

"It feels good." He caught both her ankles.

"But—"

Her protest was lost as he jerked her in. She came up shaking and sputtering, wiping her hair from her eyes. "Gee thanks. I could have hit my head on the ladder, you know."

"But you didn't." He shook his head, showering her with water. Like miniature diamonds caught by the sunlight, droplets glistened in his beard and his soft dark hair.

Soft. Carly wasn't sure how she knew his hair was soft. She longed to confirm the feeling. *Longed?* Yes, she admitted to herself, being with Ben filled her with longing. Each day she longed for him to arrive. Then she longed for him to stay. And right now, as he smiled at her, she longed to know how his mouth would feel against her own.

Cheeks stinging with color, she dove and struck out for deeper water. Steady, sure strokes carried her away from the source of her confusion. No matter how often she had wished to feel like this again, she wasn't prepared for her desire to be so strong, so disconcerting.

Ben caught up with her easily. Every time she swam away, he appeared at her side. Finally, in exasperation, she asked the question that had been on the tip of her tongue for days. "What does your houseguest think about all the time you're spending over here?"

"Oh, that's no problem."

"But surely she—"

"She?" Ben cocked an eyebrow. "Did I say my guest was a she?"

"I just assumed so."

"That's dangerous business."

"What?"

"Assuming," he said, smiling again.

Before she could press him for an answer, he disappeared beneath the surface once more, and in a moment Carly felt herself being tugged under, also. She twisted away, and a heated chase ensued. She forgot everything but how good it felt just to have fun. She pushed her muscles to their limits, trying to evade Ben's grasp. She laughed when he caught her and swallowed half the lake in the process. When he pounded her on the back she forgot to worry about being touched. At the moment nothing seemed to matter. Nothing but the sun overhead, the water against her skin, the flawless gray of Ben's eyes.

It was only when Carly climbed the ladder on the side of the dock that she realized Ben still hadn't told her anything about his guest. Grabbing her beach towel, she draped it around her shoulders and tossed an accusation at him. "I don't think you even have a houseguest."

Ben paused at the top of the ladder. "There you go. Assuming again."

"I wouldn't have to if you'd tell me."

"Share your towel, and maybe I will." He stepped onto the dock, then teasingly he caught the edges of the towel and pulled, bringing Carly close in the process.

He was mere inches away from her. Near enough for Carly to see the laughter leave his eyes. Close enough for him to lift a hand to her chin. Yesterday or the day before, the touch might have alarmed her. But not today. Today, she stood silently and still. Waiting. For what she wasn't sure.

It took all of the patience Ben had learned in the past eight years to merely stand there. Had he ever wanted to kiss a woman as much as he wanted to kiss Carly? That didn't seem possible. But he knew if he kissed her, she would disappear again, and all the ease they had built between them in the past few days would go, as well.

Finally he drew away and forced a slight smile. "Don't I get a towel, too, Miss Savoy?"

She stepped back, her eyes very wide and very brown. "Of course."

He caught the towel as it fell from her shoulders. Then he turned, breaking the spell their locked gazes seemed to have conjured up. He lifted the towel to his face and took a deep breath. It smelled like her. Like sunshine and some unidentifiable perfume. Like sweetness itself. The images the smell evoked were erotic and forbidden to him. He slid the towel down his chest and sent his gaze skyward, trying not to think of her sun-warmed skin and trembling pink lips.

Carly had retreated to the end of the dock in search of another towel. But instead, she stood spellbound, watching the movement of the cloth that Ben passed over his body. Down his broad, hair-whorled chest. Across his strong shoulders. Over one leg. Then the other. He bent forward and the denim of his wet cut-offs stretched and molded itself to the contours of his firm behind.

Desire spiraled through her. Simple, basic lust. Carly had known the feeling before. For a moment she greeted it in the way she might welcome an old long-lost friend. Then Ben glanced up, catching her eye. The dock felt too small. The air between them too heavy to breathe. And Carly realized she didn't know what to do about her feelings. Who was supposed to make a move here, anyway? Did she want movement? God, what were the rules? It had been so long since she'd played the game.

When it seemed a lifetime had passed, she grabbed a towel and forced a laugh as she turned away. "Look at me, just standing around when I've got a million things to do.''

Ben remained where he was, not saying a word. His silence made her more nervous than ever, and her hands shook as she secured the towel around her waist.

"It's Friday, so Diana and the boys are coming to spend the night, and I've got a grill to clean and food to prepare.'' Carly knew she was chattering, but she couldn't help herself. She scurried around the dock, unnecessarily unfolding lawn chairs and talking nonsense while she avoided looking at Ben. If she talked long and hard enough, perhaps she could ignore the weakness in the pit of her stomach.

"Carly.''

Her back to him, she paused in the boathouse doorway. She took a deep breath, squared her shoulders and turned around with the brightest smile she could muster. It faded as she watched Ben tug his T-shirt over his head. Had she always reacted so strongly to the male body? Or was it just Ben's body that interested her?

He slicked his wet hair behind his ears. "I'll be shoving off. Since you're so busy.''

Her mind was blank. "Busy?''

A line appeared between his eyebrows. "With Diana coming and all.''

"Oh,'' she murmured as realization struck. "Oh, right. I am busy.'' Politeness made her ask, "Would you like to stay for dinner?'' Just as politely, he declined. Carly wasn't sure if she was disappointed or relieved.

After pushing his feet into the shoes he had discarded, Ben started toward the cabin. "I'll just collect our tools from the roof."

Carly caught up with him, feeling compelled to fill in the silence. "Do you want to finish the roof tomorrow?"

His hesitation was slight but noticeable. "Maybe. Let's keep it loose, okay?" With only a casual flip of his hand he went around the side of the house to the ladder. Carly had nowhere to go but inside.

Once there, she went straight to the bathroom, stripped and stood under the lukewarm spray of the shower. Like someone awakening from a deep sleep, her every nerve ending tingled. The sensation reminded her of those days in the hospital after the attack. She had spent so much time in a drugged haze that the pain, when it came, had been overwhelming. But in a sense, she had been happy to feel it. It meant she had survived. And she had been thankful... for a little while... until the fear set in.

Now Ben made her feel alive.

He made her glad they hadn't killed her.

Unconsciously Carly's fingers traced the scar that sliced her stomach from left to right. From just beneath her breast to below her navel. The other scars had faded to almost nothing. The bruises were long gone. The bones had mended. This one scar, however, remained. A physical reminder of the horror. As if she needed more than her memories.

Choking back a sob, she lifted her face to the water. *No,* she told herself, *I'm not going to cry. This isn't worth crying about anymore.* Instead of dwelling on the past, she thought of what had happened today. Of the way Ben had looked standing in the sunlight. Of the way his smile made her feel.

And the tears didn't come.

For some people the victory might have been small. For Carly it was huge. In months past the tears had always come, no matter how strong she tried to be or how hard she fought them. Her inability to control her emotions had been the most frustrating effect of her ordeal. It had disturbed her much more than the broken ribs or the scar. She had always been so certain of herself, in charge of her own destiny. How demoralizing it had been to think that an hour or so in a deserted building with a group of monsters could rob her of her strength.

She wasn't deluded into thinking the past was buried forever. But she had taken a giant step forward. When she shut off the water, she felt as if she had cleansed much more than her body.

Her inner peace must have shown in her face, because when Diana arrived, her first words were, "What's happened?"

"And hello to you, too," Carly shot back, taking the picnic basket her sister handed her.

"But you look fantastic."

Carly glanced down at her old aqua shorts and stretched-out T-shirt. "Really?"

"It isn't the clothes, silly." As she climbed out of the boat, Diana gave her a sharp look. "You've been spending time with Ben Jamison, haven't you?"

"Oh, for goodness sake," Carly retorted, even as she silently cursed Diana's perception. Not pausing to answer the question, she turned instead to her nephews, who had also clambered out of the boat. "Come on, you guys. I've got burgers ready for the grill."

The rest of the evening was given to dinner and the myriad demands of an eight- and ten-year-old. The next morning was equally busy, and Carly managed to avoid any more questions. When Diana and the boys left for a Little League baseball game, Carly breathed a sigh of relief. She waved goodbye and settled down for an afternoon of sunbathing with a thick juicy novel for company. She couldn't say why, but she didn't particularly want to discuss Ben Jamison with her sister.

As if there was really anything to discuss. So he was attractive. So they were aware of each other in some subtle sexual way. At least she thought they were.

Without having read a page, Carly put her novel down and, frowning, gazed across the cove to his house. She believed Ben had become aware of her yesterday. Or maybe she just wanted to think he had noticed her in the same way she had noticed him. Maybe the way he had lifted her chin had been nothing. His face didn't give much away. Still, she had felt *something* in the air between them. Maybe Ben had sensed how she was feeling and had been embarrassed, even put off. Maybe that explained why he had left so quickly.

And maybe she should stop obsessing about the man.

"That's right," she murmured. "Stop it." For even if Ben was interested in her, she didn't know if she was ready for anything more than simple awareness. And if he was interested, and if she was ready, there remained the matter of his mysterious houseguest.

Realizing she was still obsessing, she sighed in disgust and reached for her suntan lotion. She smoothed on the thick, coconut-scented cream and told herself to grow up. She also kept an eye on the opposite shore, hoping to see Ben's canoe or the small outboard he sometimes used.

It was the latter that appeared midafternoon. But Ben was nowhere to be seen. The older man who held the rudder of the motor called a friendly greeting as he swung the boat alongside her dock.

Carly stood and slipped into the oversize shirt she used for a beach cover-up. She was pleased that the sight of a stranger in Ben's boat aroused curiosity instead of panic, but that didn't explain who he was. Catching the line he threw to her, she secured his boat and waited for an introduction.

"So you're Carly," he said as he stepped lithely from the boat to the dock. He held out a hand. "Stefan Scolari."

Accepting his strong handshake, she waited for some further explanation.

He laughed. The lines around his mouth showed just how often he gave in to amusement. "So Ben hasn't told you about me?"

"No," she replied, puzzled. "Should he have?"

"Since he's left me sitting alone these last few days, I did think he might have told you about his guest."

"His guest?"

"Me."

This charming, white-haired gentleman was a far cry from the redhead Diana had envisioned as Ben's houseguest. Thinking of the way Ben had teased her yesterday, Carly decided she'd been had.

"I thought we should meet," the man said. "Ben had to go do something at that business of his." He made an airy gesture in the direction of the lake.

"You mean the tackle shop and restaurant."

"Whatever." The man shrugged. "Ben spends so little time there, I usually forget he owns the place."

"Well, he doesn't talk about it much," Carly agreed. But then, as she had already acknowledged, Ben spent little time talking about himself. In all the hours they had spent together, they had discussed the roof and her family. They had conducted a spirited debate on spy novels and compared the merits of various soft drinks. She still knew nothing about his past or what he had done before moving here. She trusted him without knowing the usual background information one person learned about another. The man standing in front of her, however, might be able to fill in the gaps.

Before she could ask any questions, he drew her hand through the crook in his arm and began strolling toward the path. His touch was firm but non-threatening. Carly found herself smiling into his warm, brown eyes.

"I must say," he murmured, "Ben didn't tell me you were quite this lovely."

The compliment caught her off guard. With her hair scooped back in a barrette and her face smeared with coconut oil, Carly felt something less than lovely. Especially next to this man with his elegant manners and obviously expensive clothes. His sandals looked like real leather. His watch had probably cost more than her yearly salary. He seemed to be a man who was used to taking charge. He wasn't at all the sort of person she would imagine T-shirt-clad Ben having as a guest or friend.

"Perhaps you could offer me a glass of iced tea," he said as they climbed the path to the cabin. "I've found that tea here in the South has a completely different flavor than anywhere else in the world. Why is that, do you know?"

He was so very smooth that Carly didn't think twice about inviting him into her home. They sat on the porch. She poured tea. He made effortless, amusing conversation. Eventually the polite talk turned slightly more personal.

"You're a schoolteacher, right?" Stefan—as he'd insisted she call him—asked.

"A principal, not a teacher," she corrected. "I believe you have me at a distinct disadvantage. Ben may have told you about me, but I don't know a thing about you."

He chuckled and straightened the crease in his well-pressed khaki walking shorts. "I'm not very interesting." He took another sip of his tea. "This, by the way, is wonderful. Do I detect a slight taste of orange?''

"It's my stepmother's influence. She always adds orange juice to her tea. But as I said—"

"Yes, we were talking about you, weren't we?"

"Actually—"

"So you live in New York City?"

"I'm sure Ben has told you where I live."

"But the boy never has been good with details."

"Boy?" she repeated, amused that anyone would refer to Ben that way. He was so very much a man. "It sounds as if you've known him for quite some time."

Stefan's smile was enigmatic.

She sighed in frustration. "I'm beginning to think you and Ben both have something to hide. I've never met two people so disinclined to talk about themselves."

"Perhaps we just don't want to bore you."

"You can stop talking if I start to yawn."

He laughed. "You are charming. I think I understand why Ben has spent so much time over here."

Carly flushed. "We've been working on the roof."

"Oh, yes," Stefan murmured, his eyebrows lifting skeptically. "The roof would be an attraction, yes."

"Ben does seem to enjoy the work."

"He's developed a curious affection for manual labor since moving here."

"You don't approve?"

Without answering, Stefan set his glass on the table and stood, moving to gaze at the view of the lake. "It is beautiful here, isn't it?" he said at last.

"This is the most gorgeous place I've ever been in my life," Carly said, resigned to not gaining any information about Ben from him.

Hands in his pockets, Stefan leaned one shoulder against the rough-hewn log that framed the screened window. He drew a pack of cigarettes from his front pocket. "And what other places have you seen?" The question, which could have been derisive, was merely curious.

She smiled and declined his offer of a cigarette. "I guess I haven't seen too many places. Certainly nowhere exotic. But I still think this view would stack up against most of the ones you could offer."

There was a click and the smell of smoke as Stefan lit his cigarette and took a deep draw. He regarded Carly solemnly. "Something tells me this view is colored by your memories. Childhood memories?"

"So Ben *has* told you all the details."

"Merely that you stayed here as a child."

She nodded. "That's why I wanted to come back. I kept remembering how happy we all were here."

"And you wanted to be happy again?"

She glanced at her companion sharply. "I didn't say I wasn't happy."

Again that knowing smile played about his lips. "No, you didn't. That's what Ben said." Without pausing for her to react, he pushed open the screened door and went down the steps to the path.

Carly sat immobile for a moment. So Ben thought she was unhappy. Nothing startling about that observation. She hadn't been happy for a long time and hadn't particularly bothered to hide it. Her jumpiness must have told him all wasn't right with her. Perhaps what surprised her was that Ben would be discussing her with someone else. He had given her some thought. She wasn't sure why that pleased her, but it did.

She didn't pursue the thought. She got up and joined Stefan outside. With a skillfulness she could only admire, he steered the conversation away from himself and Ben and on to her. Perhaps only a half hour passed, but without revealing any specifics, he made her feel as if she had known him forever. They were immersed in a discussion of Manhattan's better points when a boat's motor called her attention to the lake. The ski boat was unfamiliar to Carly.

But not to Stefan. He laughed softly and murmured, "So Ben has tracked me down."

Carly followed him down the path, thinking that every day brought a new surprise about Ben. Today it was this sleek little ski boat. And his unexpectedly cosmopolitan and sophisticated houseguest. Ben seemed less and less like her idea of a typical tackle-shop owner. She had decided he might be a throwback to the sixties, someone who wanted to live next to nature. But now her imagination conjured up major crime syndicates and their leaders. The closer Ben's boat came to the dock, the faster she jumped to conclusions.

As he guided the boat in, Ben told himself he should have expected to see Stefan standing there with Carly. The man had been pumping him for information about her, giving him those knowing little smiles, encouraging him to spend his time with her. It stood to reason Stefan's natural curiosity would bring him across the cove. There was no reason to be bothered. Except that Stefan was his only link with the old Ben. The man would never betray Ben's confidences. Yet it seemed somehow important that Carly never know about his old way of life.

When had she become so important to him?

They barely knew each other. Given all that he had to hide, they would probably never really know each other. In those moments when he was thinking clearly, Ben told himself he would finish the roof and then leave Carly Savoy alone for the rest of the summer. She would leave, and he would go back to his solitary life. Unfortunately the more time he spent with her or spent thinking about her, the less clear minded he became and the harder it was to stay away. Especially when they had moments like yesterday, when a lightning rod could have been used to measure the electricity between them.

Whether he continued to spend time with Carly or not, when she was gone he would be not merely alone, but indescribably lonely. That was what happened when someone reminded you that you were alive.

Maintain your cool, he told himself as he killed the boat's motor. He put a smile on his face as he stepped onto the dock. "So I see you've met my guest," he said to Carly. Instead of smiling back, she regarded him with something like suspicion. Ben frowned, wondering why.

Stefan spoke up. "I decided I was tired of looking at the view and smoking on my own. I came over here to meet your neighbor."

"Yes, *he's* not what I expected," Carly murmured.

Another smile failed to elicit a response from her, so Ben turned to Stefan. "Smoking and sitting aren't the only things you could be doing, you know."

"Please don't tell me I could have fished or hiked." Stefan shuddered slightly.

Ben laughed. "Carly, this man doesn't understand what to do with himself if he doesn't have a phone plastered to his ear."

Carly had been darting glances between the two men. Now her brown eyes narrowed as she surveyed Stefan's face. "So you do a lot of business on the phone?"

"Most civilized people do," he retorted. "I can't understand how anyone can live anywhere without telephone service."

"Civilized people call it relaxation," Ben said. "Or getting away from it all."

"Or hiding out," Carly added softly.

Hiding? Alarm raced through Ben as he stared at her. *What did she mean by hiding? What did she know?* Chin lifted, she was regarding him with an expression he couldn't quite fathom.

Stefan broke the awkward silence with a smooth laugh. "I guess we're all hiding from one thing or another."

"Are we?" Carly returned. Ben thought she sounded angry.

Apparently unaware or uncaring of her sudden reserve, Stefan merely laughed again. "Yes, my dear. Everyone at one time or another feels the need to retreat from the world." He turned his gaze to Ben. "Although there are those who carry it to the extreme."

Ben frowned at him, but before he could say anything, Stefan was speaking to Carly again.

"I want you to come to dinner," he said. "Tomorrow night." He checked her protest. "Now, I won't take no for an answer. Tomorrow's my last day here. I'm flying home Monday morning."

"Home?"

"To Los Angeles."

"Oh." Carly looked surprised, but she protested again, "I really can't come—"

"Oh, but, *cara mia*." With a smile that flashed and a voice that caressed, Stefan used his charm as Ben had seen him use it so many times in the past. "Would you condemn me to another evening of gazing at that?" He pointed at Ben. "Give me some happy memories of this place. Please, I insist that you join us."

Dragon ladies had fallen before that tone. Ben knew Carly didn't stand a chance. She was grinning by the time Stefan started to leave.

"Until tomorrow," he said as he stepped down into the little runabout.

Ben leaned down as he tossed the line into the boat. "Very smooth," he whispered.

"Someday you'll thank me." Stefan flashed another smile, then busied himself starting the motor.

Frowning, Ben watched the man leave. Instead of thanks, what he wanted to give him was a firm kick in the behind.

He turned toward the cabin, steadfastly avoiding Carly's gaze. "I'm going to finish the roof," he offered in gruffer tones than he'd intended. He did his best not to look at her for the rest of the afternoon.

The next evening, however, was a different story.

From the moment Carly appeared on his dock promptly at seven, Ben couldn't take his eyes off her. Not off the shining red-gold hair that fell to her shoulders. Or the delicate sun-kissed beauty of her face.

Why did she seem so different? It wasn't really her hair or makeup. It was something in the air between them.

When Ben led Carly into the living room, even Stefan, who was used to gorgeous women, seemed impressed. He smiled and bowed over her hand, but he spoke to Ben.

"You can thank me now," he said.

And while his laughter echoed around the room, Ben thought once again about the merits of a well-placed kick.

Chapter Four

They aren't criminals.

Repeating that silently to herself, Carly made a slow turn in the middle of Ben's spacious living room. He had excused himself to check on dinner. Stefan was pouring her a glass of wine and chatting about the possibility of rain. It was all very normal. These were nice, although slightly out-of-the-ordinary, people. She was perfectly safe.

Yesterday, as they'd stood on the dock, her imagination had taken flight into a ridiculous realm. She had become convinced the two men were involved in something devious. God only knew why she had made that comment about hiding out. Ben had momentarily lost his cool mask. He had glared at her and appeared furious at Stefan's flippant attitude.

Of course, then she had allowed Stefan to charm her with his dinner invitation. She had told herself to stop being silly. But Ben had been very distant the rest of the afternoon. She had watched him warily, wondering if she had seen his face on one of those fugitive-from-the-law television programs. Perhaps that was why he had seemed so familiar at first. Maybe Stefan was a fellow escapee. They were both secretive. Neither of them seemed to belong here in Polk County, Tennessee. Stefan looked as if he should be vacationing in the south of France. She could picture Ben living the laid-back life on a beach in Hawaii or Tahiti. If they were hiding out, why had they chosen her family's quiet little cove?

It was with relief that she had said goodbye to Ben at dusk. Then she spent the evening jumping at every sound.

Sanity came with the dawn. Since the rape, Carly had looked at every stranger's face with suspicion. She had forgotten to trust the little voice deep inside that had always guided her actions. Only in the past few days had she begun to relax. Intuition had told her that Ben Jamison was someone she could trust. And if she ever hoped to regain her equilibrium, she had to go with her instincts on this one. She had once been strong, calm and sensible. She would be that way again. Starting now. Ben and Stefan weren't killers hiding out from the law.

But who in the hell were they?

"Here you are," Stefan said now, handing her a glass. "This is one of my new, most favorite wines, a California blush."

Surely dangerous criminals weren't this smooth. "New *and* most favorite?" she murmured before taking a sip.

"Wine is one of my passions, and I enjoy discovering new vintages."

Carly savored the faintly sweet taste for a moment. "I'm not an expert, but this is wonderful."

"Excellent." Stefan touched his glass to hers. "To lovely ladies."

She took another sip, pleased but embarrassed by the compliment and Stefan's admiring gaze. She had been determined to look her best tonight. From her limited wardrobe, she had chosen a full blue chambray skirt and sleeveless white eyelet blouse. Stefan was as elegantly casual as she had expected him to be. Even Ben had discarded the usual cut-offs for jeans and a white button-down. Of course, the jeans were faded and tight. His muscular legs and firm rear did wonderful things for those jeans.

"How charming to see someone who still blushes," Stefan murmured.

Flustered, she pulled her thoughts from Ben. "You are a terrible flirt."

"Terrible? I prefer to think I'm an accomplished one." Without pausing, Stefan gestured to the room. "So, what do you think of Ben's hideaway?"

Hideaway. Carly almost choked on her wine. Was Stefan playing some subtle game? His face revealed nothing more than polite interest, so she reined in her imagination again and glanced around. "It's a beautiful room," she said.

That was an understatement. Though even from a distance she had been able to tell this was no typical lakefront cabin, Carly was still surprised by this room. A massive stone fireplace dominated one wall. Another wall made solely of glass jutted at odd angles, hugged by the multilevel deck that overlooked the cove. At the end opposite, where Ben had disappeared, a staircase led to a darkened loft. Probably a bedroom, she decided.

"Why don't we go up and take a look at the view," Stefan suggested.

She turned to him, surprised. "Up?"

In answer, he started up the stairs, touching a light switch near the bottom. Carly followed somewhat warily.

The loft was like an eagle's aerie. From its windows, the entire cove was spread for the viewing. Carly's cabin. The house near the cove entrance. The lake beyond. The mountains that hovered over it all. In the early summer dusk, lights were just beginning to come on in the collection of buildings near the Lake Ocoee Inn and Marina. Clouds were gathering on the horizon, promising rain.

Enchanted, Carly was drawn to the view. "It's fantastic," she whispered.

"Thank you."

At the sound of Ben's voice, she spun around, smiling. "Did you really build this?"

Wearing an inscrutable expression, he crossed to stand beside her. "It seemed a shame to let all this go to waste."

"I'd spend all my time up here."

Chuckling, he gestured toward the rest of the space. "I'm afraid I do."

For the first time she glanced around. Unlike the picture-perfect room downstairs, this one looked lived-in. A multitude of magazines littered the coffee table and the low, well-worn couch. Plump pillows were tossed about. Against one wall was a unit containing a stereo system, a big-screen television and a VCR. Shelves held an extensive collection of videotapes.

"It looks as if you don't even need the rest of the house."

Stefan laughed. "That's exactly what I've been telling him for years."

"But I do have the rest of the house," Ben said. "Including a kitchen and a dining room where dinner is waiting."

While not as spectacular as the loft, the dining room's view was good, too. The food was even better. Crisp salad, fresh bread and fettuccine Alfredo. Compared to Carly's simple meals of crackers and soup, salads and sandwiches, it was a feast.

"So I did teach you something," Stefan told Ben after tasting the cheese-and-cream-smothered noodles.

Ben shook his head. "It's not quite as good as yours." He turned to Carly. "Stefan is an expert cook, at least when it comes to Italian dishes. When I was a boy..." He paused, as if realizing he was about to betray something about his past.

"More wine?" Stefan cut in with the ease Carly now knew to expect from him.

But she wasn't following his lead this time. "So you and Stefan have always been friends?" she pressed, watching Ben.

"Always," he answered.

"Since before he was born," Stefan added as he refilled Carly's wineglass.

"Before?"

The older man's eyes softened. "Ben was due any minute when I moved into the boardinghouse where his mother lived. He was acting up that day. He continued doing so for many years."

A grin tugged at Ben's lips. "I already told Carly I was rowdy." He sipped his iced tea, and for the first time Carly noticed he wasn't drinking wine.

Thinking it odd, she stared so long and hard at his glass that she missed Stefan's question. "Pardon?"

He repeated himself. "I'm sure you're used to rowdy youngsters, aren't you?"

"Rowdy?" Looking at her plate, she twirled noodles around her fork. "That's not the word that comes to mind first."

"And what does?"

"Troubled. Violent." The memories crowded at her, making her shiver. She glanced up and caught the concern in Ben's gaze.

Stefan didn't seem to sense her unease. "So your school is a tough one."

She put down her fork and took a deep breath. Part of the healing process was having normal conversations about her work. And she did care about it, deeply. At least she used to care. "It's a bad neighborhood," she explained. "We have a lot of problems with drugs. And with the gangs."

Ben frowned. "Why stay there?"

"Someone has to," Carly shot back, sharper than was necessary. "If everyone gives up, we might as well surrender the streets to the dealers and the pimps."

He held up a hand. "Sorry. I didn't mean anything—"

"No, I'm sorry." Under the table she twisted her hands together. Wringing her hands had become a bad habit. She forced herself to stop, to relax. "I get a little crazy about my work sometimes."

"I think you must be good at what you do," Stefan said slowly.

She shrugged. "Most of the time I fight a losing battle."

"And you think about giving up?"

"Two years ago I would have said no," she replied, reaching for her water glass.

"And now?" Ben pressed.

"Now I don't think every kid who takes a wrong turn can be saved."

He sat back in his chair, rubbing his beard thoughtfully. "You never really thought everyone could be saved, did you?"

"Sure I did." With as little emotion as possible, she told them about her work with students who were recovering addicts, about the community task force she had organized to fight the gang influence. "The problem is economic," she explained. "Why work hard and try for an education when you can make so much money selling drugs?"

"Yeah." Ben's mouth twisted. "Easy money."

Stefan's gaze was centered on the wine in his glass. "The names have changed. The stakes are different. But it's an old problem. I grew up in a neighborhood like you describe, Carly." His smile was slight. "In Chicago. With whores on the street corners and winos in the alleys. There, you joined a gang or you fought for your life. Even when you joined, you fought." His smile disappeared, and he looked up, his gaze skipping from Ben to Carly. "I chose to run in the end."

Arms on the table, she leaned forward. "To where?"

"To the army first." A smile touched with sadness settled on his mouth once more. "Then to Hollywood, of course. In those days, everyone with big dreams went to Hollywood. Now I think they go to Wall Street."

She could see him as he might have been then—tall and handsome and full of youthful optimism. Judging by the look of the man he had become, some of those young dreams had come true. "And what happened to you in Hollywood?" she pressed, intrigued by the story.

"Everything." Again he glanced at Ben, and his smile died. "Everything and nothing that I expected."

"But you stayed?"

He took up his wineglass again. "In Hollywood? Why, of course."

"And that's where you met Ben's mother?"

Stefan smiled his confirmation. Carly glanced at Ben. His gaze was fastened on some point far above her head, and he appeared immersed in his own thoughts.

"Well," Stefan pronounced with a note of finality. "I think that's enough nostalgia for one night. Why don't we have some coffee out on the porch?"

Carly wanted to protest. She wanted to know what had happened to him in Hollywood. She wanted to know why the mention of Ben's mother put such a bittersweet smile on Stefan's lips. If they kept talking, she was certain she'd discover what had brought Ben to this quiet cove. And that interested her most of all.

He was hiding, she decided. Just as she had expected. But not from the police. Perhaps, like her, he was hiding from the world.

Ben could almost hear the wheels spinning in Carly's mind. They sat in near darkness on the screened porch off the kitchen, so he couldn't see her face. But he knew she was taking everything that had been said at dinner, synthesizing it, trying to draw conclusions. This afternoon, Stefan had said that if she hadn't figured out who he was by now, she probably wouldn't. But she was a persistent woman. Ben had guessed that much before tonight. She had confirmed his opinion of her by the way she had talked about her work.

Drugs and gangs. They seemed an unlikely crusade for someone who looked so fragile. Yet, anyone who doubted her fervor need only to look in her face when she talked about her projects. Maybe she was a little burned-out. Perhaps the enormity of the task had dulled her initial enthusiasm. But God, how she cared. She cared as only a good person, a truly good person can care about injustice. He had respect for her dedication. Just as he shared her unwavering sense of right and wrong.

That was why he didn't want her ever to know what he had been.

While he was brooding over that, Carly stood. "I can smell the rain. I think I should get home."

"Please don't," Ben heard himself say. He swallowed, trying not to appear too eager. "I mean, the storm's close. Why don't you wait it out?" Thunder rumbled. "See? You should stay here for a while."

She argued a few minutes more but in the end was convinced to stay by another particularly violent clap of thunder and flash of lightning. The rain came soon after.

"It's a good thing my roof is fixed," Carly said.

Stefan's lighter flared in the darkness as he lit a cigarette. "Yes, since all it does on this lake is rain, it's fortunate you've fixed the leaks. I'm looking forward to getting back to the land of sunshine tomorrow."

"Sunshine and earthquakes," Ben said dryly.

"I'll take my chances."

Carly set her coffee mug on a low wooden table. "What time is your flight?"

"Too early," Stefan retorted. "And therefore, I'm going to be very rude and take myself off to bed. I don't get started the same way I used to." Taking Carly's hand, he offered his goodbyes, stood and started for the door.

What a fake, Ben thought, knowing Stefan just wanted to leave him and Carly alone. Aloud he said, "Surely you're not sleepy. I thought you West Coast power brokers could wheel and deal all night and play two sets of tennis in the morning."

"Power broker?" Carly said teasingly. "Goodness, you sound like an important man, Stefan."

He turned, silhouetted in the doorway by the muted light from the kitchen. "Don't you know? Hollywood is just like ancient Rome. And we agents are the gods. *Ciao, cara mia.*"

An agent. Sitting perfectly still, with hands clutched in her lap, Carly absorbed the information Stefan had thrown at her in such an offhand way. It suited him. Both the job and the way he had told her about it. She had done everything but stand on her head in order to get some personal details out of him, then he let it slip with studied, calculated casualness. What was it he expected her to do with the knowledge, anyway?

"I could get a complex, you know."

She looked up. For some reason she thought Ben had followed Stefan out. Instead, he stood near the front of the porch, his white shirt a pale shadow against the dark surroundings. "I'm sorry. A complex about what?"

"Stefan. The minute he left, you stopped talking."

"Is he really an agent?"

Ben's laugh was short. "And a minor god, too."

"A Hollywood agent," she murmured. "Here in our little cove. I don't know why that's so hard to imagine."

"Well, believe it." A hint of sarcasm had crept into his voice. "You can write your friends back home about it."

Carly bit her lip, wondering why Ben sounded so resentful of Stefan. Earlier they had seemed as close as father and son. "Are you glad he's leaving tomorrow?"

He paused, and even in the dim light Carly could see that he'd turned away from her. "No, I'm not glad," he finally said. "But he has this annoying tendency to try to run my life."

"I guess that comes from having known you all your life."

"Yes. He is the closest thing to a father I've ever known."

The statement was hard, a simple fact. Ben said it carelessly, as if it didn't matter. Yet it pierced Carly to the core. How did someone live without knowing their father? Even though her own hadn't been around very much, she had known him. They had a relationship. "Where was your real father?" she asked, not pausing to consider that it was the most personal of questions.

"Beats me." The speed of the answer surprised even Ben. Perhaps it was the dark intimacy of the porch, but he didn't feel like hiding everything from Carly. There were some things he could tell her.

She stood and went to his side. "That must have been hard for you."

He shrugged, staring out at the night. "Like I said, I had Stefan. Lots of people have no one."

"And what about your mother?"

Though she wasn't standing too close to him, Carly felt Ben relax. "My mother managed the best she could. In my book she was a pretty great lady."

"And Stefan was in love with her, right?"

There was a brief, startled pause. "Why do you say that?"

"There was something in his voice when he talked about her tonight."

"She didn't love him."

Another calm statement of fact. Carly wondered how much hurt this one covered.

"She should have loved him," Ben added. "He asked her to marry him dozens of times."

"Was there someone else?"

He laughed again, ruefully. "My father, I think. Can you imagine that? Loving the man who lied to you, who left you?" He turned to Carly. "She was nineteen. Pregnant. Alone in a strange city. Almost penniless. He leaves, and she loves him forever. So much for Hollywood dreams."

Carly rubbed her hand across the rough texture of the screen on the window and sighed. "I feel sorry for Stefan, but I think it would have been worse if your mother had married him without being in love."

"I think he would have made her happy," Ben insisted. "We were already a family. She could have loved him."

"You don't just choose to love."

"I know." His shoulders drooped. "I guess I've never quite let go of that particular childhood fantasy. It's like the way you remember all the things you wanted but didn't get for Christmas."

"And can never remember the stuff you got," Carly agreed.

They laughed together comfortably. Then they were quiet, and listened to the sound of the rain. It fell thick and hard. Like a curtain, Carly thought, separating them from the rest of the world. The sensation didn't bother her.

Ben finally broke the silence. "What about you, Carly? Has love ever chosen you?"

"To tell you the truth, I'm not sure."

"An interesting answer."

"I was married," she said. "I certainly thought I was in love. Even though we were both in college and had absolutely no money, I wasn't satisfied until we were married."

"Sounds pretty typical for young love."

She nodded. "God, yes. It was so impractical. I think what I wanted was a perfect little family. Probably some throwback to a forgotten trauma about my parents' divorce."

"Or so the psychologists would say."

"Exactly. Only I never remember feeling particularly traumatized. My parents were so wrong for each other.'' She sighed. ''I guess in the same way my husband and I were mismatched. My husband,'' she repeated and laughed.

''What?''

''That feels like such an odd word to apply to him. We weren't married long. And by the time it was over, I didn't feel as if I had ever loved him. He was like a stranger.''

''It's funny how that happens, isn't it?''

''What?''

He sighed. ''Two people start out with all this love. You love so hard you can't get through a day without this person. Can't make a move without their approval. And in the end you face each other like strangers. And only your lawyers talk.''

He was speaking from personal experience. Painful experience, Carly would guess, judging by the harsh tone of his voice. ''People make mistakes,'' she whispered.

''And pay for them.''

''Not forever.''

Ben looked at her. After its last, hard torrent, the rain had slackened, and already the sky seemed to have lightened. It combined with the dim light from the kitchen to reveal the gentle curves of Carly's face. She looked so very earnest. What wouldn't he give to have such optimism?

''Sometimes you have to just put the past aside. Move on,'' she said softly. Then she brushed an impatient hand through her hair. ''God, listen to me.

Here I am lecturing about letting go of the past when I—'' She stopped and shook her head.

"You what?'' he prompted.

She clasped her hands together and said nothing.

"Don't try to tell me you ever did anything terrible,'' Ben continued. "You couldn't.''

Her gaze flashed up to his. "Why do you say that?''

Embarrassed, he shuffled his feet and looked away. "You just couldn't.''

"You might be surprised.''

The affronted challenge in her voice made him smile. "Oh, really? Then tell me what deep, dark sins Miss Carly Savoy has hidden in her past.''

She didn't reply. Finally she laughed. "I guess you're right,'' she admitted. "I guess I'm just a good citizen.''

"With no skeletons in your closet. No secrets.''

Her laughter died. "I didn't say that.''

He caught the sadness in her voice. He saw her tremble. Without thinking he reached out to take her hand. She hesitated, but then allowed his fingers to curl around her own. How small her hand felt. What sweet pleasure it was to hold it in his.

"Tell me something,'' he murmured. "What brought you here this summer?''

She said nothing, and her gaze remained fixed on some point across the cove. A breeze, the coolest in days, swept across the porch, stirring her hair. Ben couldn't resist catching one of those errant strands with his free hand. Carly's eyes turned toward him then. She drew a shaky breath. Still touching the silk of her hair, he frowned a little. Why did she tremble so?

She cleared her throat. "I came here...I came to get some rest. My job..."

"Is exhausting?"

Nodding, she continued, "I was tired. This seemed like the safest place I could find."

The choice of words was telling. "Safe?"

She pulled her hand from his and turned away. "I meant peaceful."

She hadn't. She was looking for safety. Ben had only to think back to the first of the week when she had been startled by his appearance. She had screamed that first night on the dock. Carly was one very frightened lady. But why?

At this moment, reassuring her seemed more important than finding the answer to that question. "It *is* safe here. Safe and peaceful. I've been here for eight years, and nothing has ever happened." *Until you came,* he almost added. From the moment he had looked into her frightened brown eyes, his entire world had changed. He hadn't asked for the change, but it had come nevertheless. Now he wanted to protect her from whatever it was she feared.

"Carly?" Carefully, he put a hand on her shoulder. She didn't jump away as he expected. But she half turned toward him, and he sensed her wariness. "Don't be frightened," he whispered. "Nothing, no one, can hurt you here."

"I know." The words were a sigh, and the tense muscles of her shoulder relaxed somewhat under his touch. Eyes closed, she turned her head slightly, so that her cheek brushed against his hand. "With my head I know I'm safe, Ben. Really safe."

"Yes, really," he repeated. God, how soft her skin was. Soft and warm. The feel of her spread through him, seeping around corners, flooding places he thought he had sealed off forever.

How was it so? he wondered. How could she make him feel so much? Standing there in the darkness, with only the faintest of light touching her face, she looked like an angel. And surely the emotions she aroused in him came from some other-worldly source. That was the only explanation for the dead coming back to life.

As if she knew what he was thinking, she opened her eyes. Their gazes met and held. Ben sucked in his breath. There was nothing lofty or angelic about the need that surged through him at that moment. Every muscle in his body tightened.

Whispering his name, she brought her hand up to where his still lay on her shoulder. Her touch was cool. And explosive. He felt the charge everywhere.

"You..." His voice sounded hoarse, as if it had come from someone else. "You make me feel, Carly. That's the one thing I never wanted again."

"I know," she whispered. "I feel it, too. I didn't think I could."

His arm slid around her waist, drawing her close. Pulse already singing, he pressed his mouth to hers.

Like the cove, Carly thought. Ben's kiss was like the deep still waters at the center of the cove. You could dive and dive and never touch bottom. Yet you knew

it had to be there. Somewhere just beyond your reach.
As she opened her mouth beneath his, she reached for
an unnameable goal. The bottom of the cove. The end
to all her fears.

Finally he drew away, and they stared at each other
for one long, stunned moment. What was he feeling?
The light was too dim for her to read his expression.
Shadowed by his beard, his face was usually a mask,
anyway. Yet he couldn't disguise the pounding of his
heart. Or the warmth of his breath against her cheek
as he caught her close again. Carly breathed in the
scent of him. The smell of coffee and rain and some
indefinable masculine musk. Without pause, she
turned her mouth up to his once more.

He took it with less care this time. His beard was
crisp against her face. His hands were light but insistent as they pulled her closer. As his lips moved from
her mouth and down her neck, she felt the confusion
rising inside her. Like a storm cloud, it built, while she
retreated from the approaching deluge.

Ben didn't seem to notice. His mouth nibbled at her.
Tiny kisses. The sweetest of kisses, Carly told herself,
even as the darkness began racing through her.

"Kiss me."

The two words ripped into her, sharp as the knife
that had cut her flesh. And in that moment of panic,
it wasn't Ben who was kissing her. It wasn't his sweet,
tender voice that crooned her name. It was other
voices. Other hands. She could feel the gun pressed
against her head. She felt the invasion. She smelled the

sour stink of sweat as a voice whispered against her lips.

Kiss me.

The words were a whirlpool, sucking her under. She had to escape them.

"No!" With every ounce of strength she possessed, Carly pushed away from the arms that held her. Unlike those in her nightmare, these gave way easily. Unlike her tormentors, this man stepped back. Free at last, Carly fought to bring air into her lungs. She couldn't get enough air. She couldn't stop choking.

"Carly? Carly, what is it? Carly?"

The voice came from a great distance. Hands caught her again. She tried to push them away, until she felt their gentleness, until she realized it was Ben who held her, Ben who was saying her name over and over.

Horrified anew, she pushed him away again. She covered her face with her hands, fighting tears. Would she never be over this? Never be normal?

"I'm sorry," she gasped finally, when she could trust her voice at all.

"What is it? What did I do?"

There was hurt in his voice. She had never intended to hurt him. "It's me. I just . . ."

"Just what?"

Blindly, she groped for the door at the side of the porch. "It's just too fast," she managed to choke out. "We went too fast, Ben."

He stepped toward her. "I'm sorry. I didn't mean—"

"It wasn't you," she said, louder than she'd intended. "Don't you understand? It isn't you!" Her voice broke on the last word, and before the tears could fall, she pushed open the door and ran across the deck.

She fled as if the monsters of her deepest nightmares were in pursuit. Ben followed, his heart in his throat, expecting at any minute that she'd tumble on the path to his dock. But she didn't, and he didn't catch her until she was already at her motorboat. By the lights he had strung around the dock, he could see that her cheeks were wet with tears.

"You can't go like this. You're too upset."

She jerked her arm from his grasp and sat down in the boat's front seat, fumbling for the starter. "Please. Just leave me alone."

He paused with one foot on the dock, the other on the edge of her boat. The misery in her voice clawed at him. *Dear God, what had he done?* He wanted to let her go, but he also wanted to make sure she was safe. "I'll take you home," he pleaded. "Let me—"

His entreaty was cut off by the start of the engine. He had just enough time to jump back before she pulled away. White foam churned in the boat's wake, and over the roar Ben heard Carly's name being called. It took him a moment to realize the voice was his.

"What in God's name?"

Ben turned as Stefan puffed to a halt beside him. With his robe flapping in the breeze and white hair standing on end, he presented something less than his usual impeccable image. "I heard someone yelling. What happened?"

Ben started to speak and then shook his head, watching the lights of Carly's boat approach the opposite shore. How could he explain it? he wondered.

"Well?" Stefan muttered.

"I shot down an angel," Ben said at last. "Just another angel."

Turning on his heel, he left Stefan standing alone on the dock.

In her cabin, Carly threw herself onto her bed in the corner of the main room. She was shaking from the cold. She pulled the spread over her and curled into a tight, miserable ball.

God, she had thought she was ready. Dammit, she *had* been ready. She had never wanted anything the way she had wanted Ben to kiss her. Why had the nightmare caught up with her?

Tomas. Rick. Damon. Silently she repeated the names of her attackers. The men—boys, really—who had destroyed part of her. No, not destroyed, she vowed. She was battered but not beaten. They had left her for dead, but she had lived. And she had seen them punished. Now she wouldn't allow them to prevent her from living. She would conquer these fears. If it took the rest of her life, she would win.

Somehow, just telling herself that made her feel like her old self. Like the Carly who knew how to fight.

Shrugging out of the bedspread, she sat up. She wasn't going to roll up here like a whipped dog. Tonight she would get herself together. She would lie down, and she would sleep. And tomorrow she would...

She faltered for a moment but then lifted her chin. Tomorrow she would go and see Ben. Somehow she would apologize. If he walked away, well, that would hurt. But it wouldn't be the end of the world.

She didn't think so, anyway.

Finally she lay back down on the bed, praying Ben wouldn't walk away.

Chapter Five

Watching the dawn break over the cove was usually Ben's favorite way to get his day started. Particularly in the summer. Countless mornings he had sat admiring the way the sun turned the water to molten silver and the dew to a carpet of crystals. The beginning of each day was an awe-inspiring sight, one he had ignored during the first half of his life. Before moving here he had greeted many dawns, but in those days his mind had usually been on his aching head, not the beauty of the sunrise.

He saw little beauty in it today. Having given up on sleep sometime in the darkest hours of the morning, he had brewed a pot of coffee and sat alone in the loft, looking at Carly's cabin.

Her lights had burned all night, and Ben had been tempted to cross the cove to see if she was okay. What had happened? One minute she had been warm and eager in his arms. The next she had been shaking with fear. He didn't understand. He couldn't lose the image of her pale and tear-streaked face. She had been hurting. He didn't want to think he had caused her pain.

She said they had moved too fast. Yet it had been just a kiss. A powerful one, yes. But still, just a kiss. One she had wanted.

Too fast. Brooding on those words, Ben lifted the insulated pitcher and emptied the last of the coffee into his mug. Fast was a concept with which he had more than a passing acquaintance. Once upon a time he had lived in the fast lane. Money. Quick thrills. Whatever he desired he took. And lost. The losses had come faster than all the gains.

Before he could become too immersed in those memories, he heard footsteps on the stairs. Knowing it was Stefan, Ben didn't move from his chair near the window. They hadn't talked since Ben had left him standing on the dock last night. "Just don't start," he said.

"Start what?" Ben turned as Stefan nonchalantly picked up the empty pitcher, shook it and cocked an eyebrow.

"The lecture about being up all night."

"The way you spend your nights is your affair." Stefan sat on the sofa and brushed a speck of lint from his cream linen slacks. "It's none of my business.

Provided of course that you're not hurting yourself or anyone else.''

"A very mature attitude, in theory," Ben muttered and sipped the bitter liquid in his cup. He grimaced. "I'll go down and start some more coffee."

"Don't bother. We'll have to leave for the airport soon. My flight's at nine."

Ben rubbed a hand over his face. "That's right. I almost forgot you were leaving today. I'd better get ready. After not sleeping, I'm not looking forward to the drive." The nearest airport with connecting flights was about an hour away, and that was after they crossed the lake.

"I'll be ready when you are." Stefan got up and with hands shoved in pockets, gazed toward Carly's cabin. His brows were knit in a thoughtful frown.

Ben waited for him to say something. It wasn't like Stefan to keep his opinions to himself. But he didn't turn from the window, and he was curiously silent during the trip to the marina and the drive to Chattanooga.

As airports went, this one wasn't particularly large. On this Monday morning, it was busy enough, but it lacked the frantic hustle and bustle of the airports in Atlanta, New York, L.A., or a score of other cities Ben could name. It smelled the same as every other airport, however. A curious non-smell, as if too many people passed through the doors too quickly to leave anything of themselves behind. The brightly lit surroundings always made Ben nervous. Even after all these years, he still avoided crowds. He stayed away from shopping malls, and he had even been known to duck out the back door of the tackle shop when it became crowded on a Saturday afternoon.

Now he stood nervously to the side, shifting from foot to foot while Stefan checked his bag. As they started the long walk down the broad terminal corridor, he avoided meeting anyone's eyes and tugged on the brim of his baseball cap. Every seat in the waiting area near the gate where Stefan's plane would depart was filled. So they stood in the corridor, leaning against the concrete block wall.

"She isn't Angela, you know," Stefan said, finally breaking his unnatural silence.

Not looking up, Ben ground the toe of one of his worn deck shoes into the tiled floor.

"Carly isn't Angela," Stefan repeated steadfastly.

Ben knew he had to give some answer. Stefan would keep it up until he did. "She's like her."

"I fail to see the similarities."

"She's a good woman. A decent person. She thinks about others before herself, as Angela did."

"The Angela I recall didn't approach the sainthood you seem to have given her in your mind."

The contempt in Stefan's voice made Ben look at him. "You've just forgotten," he said slowly. "You've forgotten what she was like before I ruined her."

Stefan's brown eyes narrowed. "She ruined herself."

"I helped."

"She made bad choices. The same as you. Except that in the end you chose the right path. She was responsible for her own fate, Ben. You have to come to terms with that.''

Ben started to protest but decided it wasn't worth the effort. They had argued this point too many times in the past few years. ''You have your opinion, and I have mine.''

''And yours is wrong.'' Fumbling in the breast pocket of his cream blazer, Stefan produced his ever-present pack of cigarettes. ''Regardless of how our opinions of Angela differ, I agree with you about Carly Savoy. She's a good woman.''

''Which is exactly why I'm staying away from her.''

Stefan's curse was a single Anglo-Saxon word. ''Sometimes I wonder why I bother with you, Ben. You can be so dense.'' He lit the cigarette, drawing on it deeply, as if it held some life-altering message. Smoke curled through the air as he exhaled. ''Don't you see? What you need is a good woman. If you choose to live in that place, doing nothing with your God-given talents, I'd at least like to know you're not alone all the time.''

''I prefer to be alone.''

''No, you don't,'' Stefan muttered. Sadness chased the anger from his expression. ''Believe me. I know what it's like to be alone. And you don't want it, Ben.''

The pain in his eyes made Ben pause before protesting. Yes, Stefan knew something about loneliness and loss. But he didn't have Ben's demons to contend with. Or Ben's guilt.

''You don't understand,'' he said.

Stefan merely looked at him.

"I can't just take up with Carly because I don't want to be alone," Ben continued. "That's no reason to start a relationship."

"Lonely people have found themselves drawn to one another before."

"That's just it. She isn't drawn to me."

Chuckling, Stefan bent to crush his cigarette butt in the sand-filled disposal unit by his side.

"What are you laughing at?" Ben demanded.

"Your foolishness. Carly is very interested in you. If you can't see that..." Stefan raised his hand in a gesture of impatience.

Hope sparked in Ben, but the memory of the night before crushed it. Stubbornly he shook his head. "Even if she were interested, I don't deserve her."

"Don't deserve her?" Stefan repeated, clearly amazed. "Dear God, Ben, when are you going to see that you're not the same person you were ten years ago?"

"There's enough of that man left to scare the hell out of me sometimes."

"Good."

Ben looked at him in surprise.

"The problem with you ten years ago was that nothing scared the hell out of you. Now, hopefully, you have the good sense not to act on every crazy impulse."

"I'd rather get rid of the impulses."

"Oh, no." A tiny smile quirked the corners of Stefan's generous mouth. "If the impulses were gone, even the darker ones, you'd be something less than human, less than yourself."

Before Ben could make a reply, an amplified voice announced the boarding for Stefan's plane.

"That's me," the older man said unnecessarily. He picked up the small case he had dropped to the floor.

Ben straightened away from the wall, his gaze moving over the faces of the others who were gathered to board the plane. Businessmen with their briefcases open until the last minute before boarding. Vacationers with their hopeful smiles. Parents. Children. There was laughter and a tear or two.

"God, I hate airports," Ben muttered.

"No," Stefan said. "What you hate are the farewells. You always have."

The loudspeaker voice came again, calling for first-class passengers.

"You could come with me, Ben."

This was the ritual they went through every time Stefan left. Ben knew his own responses by heart, but he was never prepared for the sadness that twisted his gut. "I can't," he said now. "You know that."

Stefan nodded. His smile was tight as he gripped Ben's shoulder. "Take care of yourself."

"I will." Ben swallowed hard. "Work on not smoking, okay?"

"You sound like your mother." Smiling, Stefan took a couple of steps, but when he turned the smile was gone. "Don't give up on Carly," he said. "Promise me you'll give her a chance. Promise me you'll explore the possibilities."

"Stefan—"

"Promise? Just to please an old man."

Old. It was a word Ben had never associated with this energetic man. It was a word no one would have expected Stefan to apply to himself. Yet as he stood in that crowded airport corridor, he looked old. A little beaten. Very sad. Years ago he had saved Ben's life. If needed, he would do so again. The least Ben owed him was a simple promise.

"All right," he agreed. "I'll give her a chance."

Shoulders straightening, Stefan nodded. Then he turned and got in line for the plane. His laughter drifted back to Ben. The pink-cheeked smile of the pretty airline official checking boarding passes told him Stefan was acting like his normal self.

Ben usually left the airport at this point. Today, however, he went to the window and watched the plane pull away from the terminal. He stayed until it roared down the runway and into the sky.

Then he headed for his Jeep, thinking about his promise. He thought so long and so hard he was sure he was imagining things when, an hour later, he pulled up in front of his shop-restaurant and found Carly waiting.

She didn't see him right away. Ben considered leaving before she noticed him, but the promise he had made Stefan echoed through his mind. Seated in one of the rocking chairs that lined the shop's broad front porch, Carly was immersed in watching a man and his two young sons get into the truck that was parked a short distance away. One boy was stubbornly clutch-

ing a fishing pole, even as his father pointed out that
he had to let go of it in order to fit through the truck's
door. A soft smile touched Carly's lips as she watched
the minor struggle of wills.

God, what her smile did to a man's insides, Ben
thought. It was that smile as much as his promise that
finally propelled him out of the Jeep. As he went up
the porch steps, Carly finally glanced his way. Her
cheeks colored, but her gaze didn't falter.

Encouraged because she didn't look away, Ben
crossed the porch and sat in the chair beside hers. He
nodded toward the father and sons. "Doesn't bode
well for the rest of the fishing trip, does it?"

Some of the apprehension left Carly's eyes. "You
should have seen them in the shop. That dad may live
to regret this trip all the way around."

"So you've been in the shop. Are you thinking of
going fishing?"

"Hardly." Her smile dawned again, but she bowed
her head, rather shyly refusing to meet Ben's gaze. "I
was looking for you," she murmured.

At his continued silence, Carly dared a peek at his
expression. As usual he gave nothing away. Apolo-
gizing had seemed so easy in the safety of her cabin
this morning. Facing Ben here in the sunshine was
much more difficult. Steadfastly she set her rocker in
motion, keeping her gaze on the planked floor and her
voice very level. "I wanted to apologize for last night."

"That's what I should be doing."

"No, you didn't do anything wrong. I just—" She
bit her bottom lip, not knowing how to explain. It was

neither the time nor the place to tell him the real reasons she had become so irrationally terrified last night. That was something she didn't know if she could ever tell him, or any other man. She couldn't even discuss it with her family. But she owed him some kind of explanation for last night's hysterics, if only to settle her own mind. She tried again. "There are things that I—"

"Carly, it doesn't really matter."

His soft words made her glance up. "But—"

"You don't have to explain anything to me."

"But I want to."

"Then someday you will. Someday when it's easier." There was kindness in his gray eyes. Kindness and a gentle acceptance. "Why don't we forget last night?" he suggested.

Forgetting the kiss they shared was the last thing she wanted. Forgetting what came afterward would be a blessing. Carly gave a rueful smile. "Why is it we have to keep starting over?"

"I don't know of any rule about how many times you can start a friendship." He put out his hand. "How about it? Friends?"

She didn't really want to be his friend. And she'd bet her life that it wasn't what Ben wanted, either. She didn't know that she would ever be capable of offering him anything more. Last night's fiasco had shown her how far she had to go before she was ready for intimacy with any man. But somehow, someday, she wanted to try to be more than Ben Jamison's friend. Perhaps with time her desire would overrule the memories of that awful December night. She wanted to tell him that, but the right words didn't present themselves. So instead they sat looking at each other with what felt like a world of unspoken questions running between them.

Finally Ben released her hand and stood. "Come on. I know you've already been inside, but I'd like to show you around."

His smooth invitation broke the tension, and gratefully Carly followed him inside. She had discovered his business was something quite different than the tiny ramshackle shop she had envisioned. The building was rustic, yes, but with its front porch and rough-hewn wooden siding it had a certain charm.

"Are fishing-tackle shops supposed to be this nice?" she asked as they paused inside the doorway.

"Only if the boss does the remodeling," came the answer from across the room.

Carly turned to face the grinning man who had replaced the teenager she had found behind the counter earlier. This man's gray-streaked brown hair was thinning on top, but the ends brushed his shoulders. It combined with his salt-and-pepper beard and chubby red cheeks to make him look like one of Santa's elves. If one could imagine an elf with a Texas drawl who wore a tropical print shirt.

"Carly Savoy, meet Doc Taylor," Ben said as they crossed to the counter.

Chuckling, Doc enthusiastically pumped her hand. "I know, I know. You're wondering about a doctor who works in a tackle shop. It's a nickname. And yes,

I've got six brothers—Dopey, Sneezy, et cetera. We only thank God there was no sister for everyone to call Snow White. You can laugh now and get it over with."

They all shared a chuckle, and a woman came through an arched doorway, demanding to know what everyone was laughing about. Ben introduced her as Doc's wife, Sam. Clad in blue jeans, she was tall and slender, with the dusky skin and dark eyes that bespoke Spanish ancestry. She seemed an odd match for the shorter, plump Doc. Until she smiled. Then her eyes twinkled with the same good-natured charm he exhibited.

Both Doc and Sam seemed at ease with Ben. But Carly wasn't left with the feeling that they were close friends. They talked about the business and called him "boss." For some reason, she found that odd.

"I've got apple pie fresh from the oven in the back," Sam offered.

In a matter of minutes Carly was seated with Ben in the tiny restaurant that comprised the back half of his establishment. The space was small but pleasant, with the same rough walls and broad-planked floor as the front room. Another porch full of rockers overlooked the lake. A couple of customers were perched on stools at the lunch counter, but except for the one she and Ben occupied, the group of tables in front of the windows was unoccupied.

"Mondays are slow, even in the summer," Ben explained to Carly as Sam put two slices of pie and two coffees on the table. "But on the weekends they're lined up to sample Sam's cooking. Especially her chili."

Sam tossed off the compliment with a graceful roll of her shoulders. "No one else around here knows how to fix authentic Texas chili."

"And everyone's just glad you do," Ben said. "Try the pie, Carly. I guarantee it's great."

It was, with a flaky crust and sweetly spiced filling. Nodding her approval, Carly reached for her coffee mug. "If this is a sample of the menu, I'm going to have to come across the lake more often, Sam."

"Good. Maybe you can get the boss to eat here more often, too."

Sam sounded as if an appearance by Ben was rare. Carly wondered why.

A teenage girl called to Sam from the counter, and the woman excused herself and headed for the kitchen. Delicious, spicy aromas curled into the room before the door she'd pushed open swung shut.

"That's Sam and Doc's daughter," Ben said, indicating the girl at the counter. "Their son is renting boats down there."

Carly followed his nod to the small pier just below them, where another teenager could be seen conferring with a couple of young men. "A real family business, isn't it?"

"They're good people."

"And their boss leaves them alone."

Ben shrugged. "I don't really know much about selling bait and fishing rods or making apple pies.

Sometimes I think Doc dreads it when I offer to help out."

"So why did you buy the business?"

"It seemed like a good deal." He took a long sip of coffee. "Especially since Doc and Sam came with it."

"So they've worked here for a while?"

"They like the life, and it's not a bad way to raise their kids. There's an apartment on the second floor where the family lives."

Again Carly glanced around the room. The lunch counter and the gleaming appliances behind it looked brand new. She'd guess Ben had made a sizable investment in this place. Surely its financial rewards weren't much, especially considering it supported a family of four. His reasons for owning it intrigued her. "Besides free pie and chili, what's in this for you?"

"In it?" he repeated, frowning.

Perhaps she had been too blunt, but she was still curious. "I guess I'm asking exactly what being *the boss* entails."

Again his shrug was casual. "I balance the books, tinker with the outboards we rent, fix leaky faucets. Stuff like that."

"And that's all?"

"It doesn't sound like enough?"

Chin in hand, she looked directly into his fine gray eyes. Such intelligent eyes they were, set in his strong, handsome face. "No," she murmured. "I don't think this is enough for you."

"It's a nice life," he returned steadily. "A nice, quiet life." Picking up her mug, he went to the counter to get them more coffee.

When he returned, the Taylors' son showed up, saying there was a problem with one of the boats. Ben murmured an apology and left Carly, promising to return soon.

She sighed and finished her pie while she watched him cross the dock. The more she discovered about Ben, the more of an enigma he became. He was regarded as a son by a man who was obviously wealthy and successful. He was intelligent and attractive. Yet he had chosen a life far from the mainstream. None of it quite made sense.

Flushed and wiping her hands on an apron, Sam came out of the kitchen. She looked around in disappointment and asked for Ben. Carly explained his departure and invited the woman to join her. "You look as if you could stand a rest."

Gratefully Sam pulled out a chair and sat. "No matter what day it is, we have a regular group who come in for breakfast. And now it's time for lunch. I'm just glad it's Monday and we won't be so crowded."

Carly murmured her sympathy and wondered what Sam could tell her about Ben. As a vice-principal and counselor, she had once been good at getting people to talk. Stefan and Ben were too practiced at eluding questions to open up to even her subtle probing. Sam might be a different matter.

* * *

Half an hour later, Carly smiled in triumph as she pushed open the door to the back porch. Sam didn't really know much about Ben's background, but she had confirmed what Carly already suspected about the kind of man he was.

Carly crossed the dock and found Ben kneeling beside a dismantled outboard motor. His hair was more unruly than usual, and his cheek was smudged with the same black grease that covered his hands. Groaning, he glanced at his watch as she drew near. "I told you I'd be right back, didn't I? Sorry."

"That's okay. You looked busy. I had another piece of pie." Carly leaned against the roped fence that rimmed the dock. The sun was warm on her shoulders, but a pleasant breeze from the lake diluted its effect. She inhaled the fresh air and watched a houseboat slip past the dock. Those on board waved, and she returned the gesture, smiling happily.

Ben stood and wiped his hands on a grimy-looking rag. He squinted at her. "You look mighty pleased with yourself, Miss Savoy."

"Oh, I am."

"Was the pie that good?"

"The conversation was better," Carly returned.

His eyes narrowed in suspicion. "I learned a long time ago never to trust a woman when she looks the way you do."

She giggled. Not a laugh, but an honest-to-goodness giggle. The sound was disconcerting, even to her. How long had it been since she'd giggled? Whatever the answer, she didn't care. She just wanted to hold on to her happiness. "Can you come over this evening?" she asked Ben. "I'm going into town for groceries, and I'm in the mood for a steak. Think you could stand one?"

Still regarding her with wariness, he nodded.

"Good. I'll see you around seven." Carly turned to go, feeling lighter than air. But she took only a few steps before wheeling back to regard Ben solemnly.

"What is it?" he demanded.

She took a deep breath, and then allowed the words to rush out. "You're a nice man, Ben Jamison. You work real hard at hiding it, but you're a very nice man."

She was off like a shot, leaving Ben to stare after her in bemusement.

A nice man.

Funny how a simple compliment like that outweighed anything that had ever been written or said about him.

If he had hoped to find out what she meant, no chance came to discuss it that night. Carly's sister put in an unexpected appearance just as Ben started grilling steaks. Diana had lost her job, and having left her sons with a neighbor, she intended to spend the night.

While Diana was putting her things in the cabin, Carly outlined her sister's circumstances. It was the first Ben had heard of the divorce. "Maybe I should go," he told Carly. "She seems upset and probably just wants to talk to you."

Carly shook her head. "Diana brought this latest catastrophe on herself. I feel sorry for her, but I think it's time she stopped moping around and got on with her life." She lifted her chin. "It's time for both of us to get on with it."

There was no time to dissect her last statement. Diana appeared, and the conversation shifted to her problems. Ben could appreciate her anxiety, but this wasn't the way he had envisioned the evening. Watching Carly's delicate, flushed features across the table, he thought wistfully of the quiet stargazing he had planned. Carly in the moonlight. The combination held a special appeal. But then, so did Carly in the sunlight. Carly anywhere, anytime, was more in keeping with his real desires.

He couldn't help remembering the night before. The sweet way her cheek had brushed his hand. The softness of her hair. The smell of flowers on her skin. The taste of her lips before she had pulled away. Just the memories made him hard with need.

Avoiding her gaze, he shifted in his chair. So much for friendship. If he really meant to be her friend, he wouldn't be seated at her table with his mind full of erotic images. They clicked through his head. Carly with her mouth on his skin, her breasts in his hands, her breath catching as she opened her body to receive him...

She stood, and he pulled his mind away from the fantasy long enough to realize she was going into the cabin for dessert. He watched her leave, forgetting everything to gaze with appreciation at the rounded hips her blue jeans revealed.

Diana's soft laughter caught him off guard. "Pardon?" he asked, swinging his gaze to her.

Her green eyes were sparkling. "I didn't say anything. I was watching you watch my sister."

Ben shifted in his chair. "I didn't—"

"Don't get me wrong," Diana cut in. "I think it's great. Carly deserves to have someone watching her every move that way."

"She's an attractive woman."

A tiny frown knit Diana's brow. "Then be patient, okay?"

"Patient?"

Not quite meeting his gaze, Diana ran a finger around the rim of her coffee cup. "Carly's worth waiting for, Ben. She's...well, let's just say life hasn't done her any favors recently. So be patient."

"It's obvious something has happened to her. Something pretty terrible, I think." Ben didn't expect Diana to tell him what, but he wanted her to know he wasn't unaware of Carly's fragility. "I don't intend to hurt her."

"Somehow I knew that," Diana said softly. "But I had to say something, Ben. The world's a rotten place sometimes. Absolutely rotten."

From the doorway, Carly's voice sang out, "If that's supposed to be an earth-shattering observation, Diana, you've missed the mark." She gave no indication she had heard more than Diana's last remark. "Now come on, I need both of you to help me demolish this chocolate cake. Otherwise I'll probably eat the whole thing myself after you leave.''

So they shared cake and coffee and conversation. For hours they sat on the porch, laughing, discussing everything from where Diana was going to find a job to old rock and roll and Clint Eastwood movies.

For Carly it was a chance to see Ben in a new light. Certainly during the past week they had talked, but he had never been as open as he was tonight, not even with Stefan, whom he knew so well. Was it Diana's gregarious nature and charming manner that put him at ease? Maybe. Carly, however, felt no jealousy. How could she when Ben saved his warmest, most intimate smiles for her? Comfortably their hands collided while reaching for a second piece of cake. Even their laughter seemed to blend in a pleasing harmony.

If only she hadn't run away last night, she thought. She should have stayed and fought her fears. The next time would be different. And there would be a next time, she promised herself.

It was late when she walked Ben down to the dock. As they neared his boat, he took her hand. It felt natural. As did the shiver his touch sent through her. Silently they faced each other in the soft summer moonlight. Carly wanted him to kiss her. She wanted to prove to him and to herself that she wouldn't bolt like a frightened deer.

But he made no move to do more than touch her hand. Ben wondered if Carly felt what an effort it was to confine himself to those simple actions. Perspiration collected on his brow as he held himself in check.

Sweet heaven, just looking at a woman hadn't sent him into this state since he'd been nineteen.

He cleared his throat. "How about tomorrow?"

"What about it?"

"I thought I might do something about those squeaking doors in your house."

"Then I could fix some lunch."

"We could take the boat out."

"Maybe for a picnic."

"Yeah."

"Good. I'll fix chicken."

"And bring the cake."

The breathless, inane conversation was no more than a transparent attempt to postpone his departure. Knowing that, Ben laughed and stepped away. "I'll see you tomorrow."

"I'll be waiting."

Waiting. The sweetest, damnedest word in the English language, Ben decided as he headed back across the cove. He wanted to think of her here waiting for him, because waiting for Carly to conquer her fears was going to be the biggest challenge he had ever faced.

Chapter Six

Sighing happily, Carly lifted her face to the sun. The day was hot and humid. Somewhere people were glaring at the sky and mopping their brows. But here on her inner tube, floating down the Hiwassee River, she felt lazy and content. She was warm, but if the heat became too intense, she had merely to slip into the deep, cool waters.

"This," she said to Diana, who floated nearby, "is the way every summer day should be spent."

Her sister smiled her agreement. "If only I were rich. Then I could spend every day exactly as I pleased."

"And how would you spend them?"

"Any way that doesn't include an ex-husband, a ringing telephone or a stack of forms to be typed."

The bitter note in her voice dismayed Carly. Yesterday Diana had found a new job, another secretarial position that would begin on Monday. Carly had urged her to continue looking until she located something she found more appealing, but Diana indicated she couldn't afford to wait. The offer of a loan and the suggestion that their father would be willing to help had met with rejection, also. Diana said she was tired of being dependent on others.

She was tired of more than that, Carly decided, watching her sister with concern. There was something going on that Diana wasn't revealing. Late yesterday afternoon she had arrived unannounced at the cabin with her oldest son, J.D. She and the boy, who normally shared his mother's sunny disposition, had been subdued. Her younger son was with his father. Beyond that and the news of her job, Diana had little to say. Hoping to shake her out of the doldrums, Carly had invited her and J.D. along on this trip down the Hiwassee River with Ben.

Ben hadn't been thrilled. Carly smiled, thinking of the way he had said he preferred being alone with her. She looked ahead to where he floated beside Diana's son. He and the youngster seemed to be getting along quite well. For the hour or so they had been in the river, the two of them had been in an intense discussion of whether they were likely to see any snakes. Reptiles were one of J.D.'s consuming passions.

"Please," she called to them, "I don't want to hear anything more about water moccasins. You're spoiling my trip."

"Oh, Aunt Carly," J.D. said, "snakes are more scared of us than we are of them."

"You obviously don't understand just how frightened of the disgusting creatures I am." Shuddering, she looked toward the riverbanks. At any moment she expected to see a snake undulating through the water.

"Don't worry," Ben said, grinning as he apparently read her mind. "I think there are too many people on this river for any snakes to be interested."

It was crowded. More so than Carly had expected for a Thursday afternoon. She knew the summer brought big crowds for the white-water rafting on the more turbulent Ocoee River, but she had assumed the relatively gentle Hiwassee wouldn't be as popular. She was wrong. Tourists and locals parked their cars well down the river at Webb's Store near Reliance and climbed aboard buses and flatbed trucks for the trip up to the starting point. The float downstream got a little rocky in spots, but not enough to worry anyone who was a moderately good swimmer. Maybe it was the easiness of the trip and the river's relief from the heat that had produced today's crowd.

Carly knew the swarm of people had made Ben uneasy at first. She had seen the way he tugged at his ever-present baseball cap and ducked his head. She didn't believe he had looked directly at anyone at Webb's. Once again, while they were waiting to board the truck, he had whispered that he wished they were back at the cove. Just the two of them.

The deep, intimate sound of his suggestion, spoken close to her ear, made Carly wish for the same thing. If Diana and J.D. hadn't been along, she might have taken him up on the offer to go home.

For two weeks, it *had* been just the two of them. Oh, they had gone over to the restaurant to sample Sam's chili, and the neighbors who lived in the cove's other cabin had stopped at her dock last Sunday, but for the most part they had been alone. Alone and content.

Well, she amended, maybe not exactly content. It was hard to be satisfied when a mere glance from Ben could unsettle her. And when they touched... God, the most accidental brush of their hands made her catch her breath. If only she could be sure how she'd feel if their relationship went further. The last thing she wanted was a repeat of the night Ben had kissed her. But if only he would kiss her again.

He had come close. In the darkened comfort of his loft where they had watched an old romantic movie. On his boat or her dock, where they spent most warm sunshiny days. In the cabin where they had worked together, caulking windows and repairing rain-damaged ceilings. The opportunities had been too numerous to count. The desire had been there, too. She had read it in his eyes, seen it in the way he turned sharply away. She wanted to take his hand, to tell him what had happened to her. But something held her back.

Why? she wondered. She knew Ben had his own tragedies to contend with. Even though he carefully didn't discuss the specifics of his past, a person would have had to be blind to miss the pain that sometimes filled his eyes. Yes, Ben had known problems and probably heartbreak. There was every reason to expect he would understand what Carly had been through. Each day she trusted him, liked him, a little more. Maybe it went beyond *like*. She certainly felt attracted to him. And she was beginning to depend on his being there every day.

But still she couldn't tell him about the rape.

She was afraid the knowledge would change their relationship. After all, it had changed the way everyone else dealt with her. Friends, colleagues, students, family—all of them had tiptoed around her, as if at any moment they expected her to shatter into a million pieces. Her mother and stepfather, in their usual no-nonsense style, had tried to act as if nothing at all had happened. Diana and Margo had fussed. Her brother Sullivan had been enraged. And her father...

Carly swallowed, her eyes filling with tears as she remembered how destroyed he had looked. Thinking she was asleep, her father had sat beside her hospital bed and cried. Finally she had ended up comforting him, instead of the other way around. Even after a year and a half, none of them had ever again treated her as if she were whole. Perhaps that was the reason she'd had so much difficulty putting it all behind her. How could she forget when no one else had?

"Hey, you."

The exclamation broke into her thoughts, and she turned to meet Ben's gaze. He had propelled his inner tube close to hers and was studying her with concern.

"Stop looking like that," he ordered.

Blinking her unshed tears away, Carly forced a smile. "Like this?"

"No, but that's much better." He returned her grin and reached across the water to catch her hand in his. "Beautiful ladies should always smile."

Carly didn't protest. She accepted the compliment the same as she accepted the touch of Ben's hand— gladly. She didn't want the easiness that had developed between them to end. Even though Ben must have known something had happened to her, she was afraid if he found out the whole story he'd pull back. Worse, he might look at her with wariness or pity, just as others had. Either way, she didn't think she could bear it.

Refusing to consider the possibility, she tightened her hand in his and turned her face again to the sky. Why think the worst when the day was so beautiful, when this gentle, caring man was beside her?

The day was a hit with everyone. By the end of their trip downstream, Diana was more at ease. J.D. was a bit disappointed at not catching something slithery to take home, but the shadows were gone from his green eyes. Because J.D. begged them, Carly and Ben decided to accept Diana's invitation to dinner at her home in Cleveland instead of going straight back to Lake Ocoee. They followed her car in Ben's Jeep.

ACCEPT FOUR BRAND NEW

YOURS

We'd like to send you four free Silhouette novels, worth $11.80, to introduce you to the benefits of the Silhouette Reader Service™. We hope your free books will convince you to subscribe, but that's up to you. Accepting them places you under no obligation to buy anything, but we hope you'll want to continue your membership in the Reader Service.

So unless we hear from you, once a month we'll send you six additional Silhouette Special Edition® novels to read and enjoy. If you choose to keep them, you'll pay just $2.74* each—a saving of 21¢ off the cover price. And there is *no* charge for delivery. There are *no* hidden extras! You may cancel at any time, for any reason, just by sending us a note or a shipping statement marked "cancel" or by returning any shipment of books to us at our cost. Either way the free books and gifts are yours to keep!

ALSO FREE!
VICTORIAN PICTURE FRAME

This lovely Victorian pewter-finish miniature is perfect for displaying a treasured photograph—and it's yours *absolutely free*—when you accept our no-risk offer.

Perfect for a treasured Photograph

Plus a FREE mystery gift! follow instructions at right.

*Terms and prices subject to change without notice.
Sales taxes applicable in New York and Iowa.
© 1990 HARLEQUIN ENTERPRISES LIMITED*

SILHOUETTE SPECIAL EDITION® NOVELS

FREE!

 Silhouette Reader Service™

```
AFFIX
FOUR FREE BOOKS
STICKER HERE
```

YES, send me my four free books and gifts as explained on the opposite page. I have affixed my "free books" sticker above and my two "free gift" stickers below. I understand that accepting these books and gifts places me under no obligation ever to buy any books; I may cancel at anytime, for any reason, and the free books and gifts will be mine to keep!

235 CIS R1YU (U-SIL-SE-09/90)

NAME
_____
(PLEASE PRINT)

ADDRESS _____ APT. _____

CITY _____

STATE _____ ZIP _____

Offer limited to one per household and not valid to current Silhouette Special Edition® subscribers. All orders subject to approval.

```
AFFIX FREE
VICTORIAN
PICTURE
FRAME
STICKER HERE
```

```
AFFIX FREE
MYSTERY GIFT
STICKER HERE
```

PRINTED IN U.S.A.

Diana's house was in one of the growing town's newest and most affluent subdivisions. Two-storied and beautifully landscaped, the house had a basketball hoop over the garage door and a swing set out back. It appeared to be a dream house for the perfect family. But Carly saw the discordant reminders of the broken dream. The For Sale sign in the front yard. The bills stamped Past Due stacked so neatly on Diana's desk in a corner of the roomy kitchen. Then there was the sports car that pulled into the driveway carrying Diana's ex-husband, their younger son and an unidentified woman. The harshest note of all was the way J.D. retreated to his room and refused to speak to his father.

Carly thought Diana handled it all very well. She was polite. With a hand on her youngest's shoulder, she calmly watched her ex-husband and his friend leave. She coaxed J.D. to the table and they ate. Only when it was over and the children were out back did she sit at the table, head bowed, as if the weight she carried was too heavy. Jim was remarrying in another week. J.D. was refusing to accept the idea. His brother didn't seem to understand the significance of the step. He still talked about what would happen when his daddy came home. Perhaps Diana had encouraged that, because she still couldn't grasp that she'd lost the battle for the man she loved.

Fighting tears, Diana faced Carly and Ben and asked what she had done wrong, why Jim didn't love her, what she could do to keep him from making what she was certain was a horrible mistake. That she would come so unglued in front of someone she didn't know well told Carly just how distraught her sister was. Ben tactfully left them alone and went out to shoot baskets with the boys, but Carly didn't really have any words of comfort for Diana. She offered to stay the night, but Diana wouldn't hear of it.

Depressed over the whole affair, Carly was silent as Ben turned down Waterlevel Highway toward the lake. After several moments, he placed his hand where hers rested on her leg. The touch was warm and comforting, not in the least threatening. Gratefully she threaded her fingers through his.

"Think she'll be okay?" he asked.

Carly sighed. "I guess there aren't any guarantees. I just wish Diana could work through her bitterness."

"She seems to have reason enough for being bitter."

"It's a two-way street. Much as I love my sister, the end of the marriage can't have been Jim's fault alone."

"She still cares for him."

"And feels responsible for him," Carly added. "She's got to get over that."

"It isn't so simple." The sharpness of his tone made Carly look at him in surprise. "The man's a damn fool, in my opinion. It looks to me as if he's thrown something pretty special away. With Diana. Especially with his kids. Can you imagine what it must feel like to have your son look at you that way?" Ben sucked in his breath. "At least Angela and—" He broke off and dropped her hand to downshift as a car pulled into their lane.

"Angela?" Carly murmured. She felt Ben's hesitation. Even though the Jeep was dark and she couldn't make out his expression, she could feel the way he stiffened. "Who is Angela?"

"My wife."

Carly felt as if all the air had been forced from her lungs. "You're married?" she managed at last.

"Was," Ben supplied quickly. "Was married. A long time ago. Eons ago." Funny, but it had never seemed so long ago until this moment. His memories of Angela had always been so near, so painfully close.

He spared a glance from the road to Carly. Lights from passing cars washed over her face. She was sitting still and quiet, her gaze fixed straight ahead. "You seem surprised," he said when the silence between them had stretched too tightly for him to bear.

She shook her head. "I'm not. Not really. But..."

"What?"

"It's just the way you answered at first. As if she were still your wife."

"I didn't mean for it to sound that way. It was over between us ten years ago. And then—" he bit his lip then plunged ahead "—then she died." He swallowed. "She killed herself."

Carly's indrawn breath seemed to ricochet around the small vehicle. Not looking at her, Ben gripped the steering wheel as hard as he could. He pressed the accelerator down, too, until the Jeep was hurtling through the summer night.

It had been another summer when he'd learned Angela was dead. He had spent the evening with some woman. She had eased the hunger of his body and left him alone in a shabby motel room in Montana. Or had it been Wyoming? All he really remembered was the smell of cheap perfume, the rattle of the newspaper as he'd turned the pages, and finally the bitter acid of regret that had burned his throat when he read the small, easily missed item at the bottom of a page.

God, he had wanted to escape that night. He had wanted something, anything that would chase the devils out of his head. But instead of searching for some magic cure, he had driven, just as he was driving now. And the road he had taken had eventually led him to this quiet corner of the world.

"Ben?" Carly's voice was soft. Her touch on his arm was gentle. It brought him back to reality and forced him to ease up on the gas.

"Sorry," he muttered. "I didn't mean to scare you."

"You didn't." Her hand tightened on his arm. "You're okay, aren't you?"

Was he? He turned his face to the open window. The wind blew in his face. It smelled of just-mown grass. Fresh. Clean. Real. Up ahead was the dam that had been built to form Lake Ocoee. He remembered how he had felt the first night he had stood on the overlook beside that dam and smelled this air and looked at the lake in the moonlight. He had promised himself then that he wouldn't spend the rest of his life with regrets. By hiding away here, he had hoped to avoid the temptations that had once nearly destroyed him. He wouldn't make the same mistakes. Most importantly he would never put himself in the position of hurting someone else the way he had hurt Angela.

But on that night, he hadn't dreamed there'd be Carly.

Oh, as Stefan had said, he wasn't the same man who had left Angela alone in Los Angeles to fight her own battles. There were mistakes he had made that wouldn't be made again. But a voice, a tiny reminder deep inside him, said he wasn't what someone like Carly needed. He wasn't whole. He wasn't good.

Yet he wanted her.

Not just physically, although that long, ceaseless ache was part of the whole picture. He wanted to be close to her, to share with her in a way he hadn't shared with anyone. And he wanted her to want him. That's what the past few weeks of patient, gentle wooing had been about. He wanted, *needed* her to face him, to come to him without fear.

"Ben, are you okay?" Carly repeated.

They were rounding the bend near the dam. He glanced at the moon-dappled water and turned to her. "I'm okay," he whispered. "And I think it's your fault."

"You make it sound like a mistake."

"Maybe it is. Maybe *we're* a mistake. But I can forget that when I'm with you."

For a moment there was only the sound of the Jeep as its wheels hugged the lakeside road. Then, her voice hushed, Carly said, "You make me forget things, too, Ben. Painful things."

"So maybe we're good for each other?"

"Maybe."

Before the road dipped to the right, Ben turned the Jeep into its usual slot next to the restaurant and tackle shop. He cut the motor and reached for Carly all in the same fluid movement.

She slipped into his arms easily, the way movies and books said a woman ought to but seldom did. Just as she had on that night she had run away, she felt as if she belonged there next to him. Her lips slanted under his. They opened. Answered. Accepted. How sweetly she gave.

Where had she been? That corny line was all Ben could think of as Carly melted against him. But it did seem a shame that he had spent such long, lonely years without knowing what it was to kiss her. If Carly had been his long ago, perhaps he wouldn't have made such a mess of his life. Yet perhaps it was because he knew what hell looked like that he could recognize perfection.

Yes, it was perfect. She was perfect. Groaning at the delicious agony that holding her aroused in him, Ben deepened the kiss. He grew hard. He kissed her with barely restrained desperation. Carly didn't pull away. If anything, she matched his ardor. Gently he slipped his hands through her hair. He turned toward her, trying to bridge the space the bucket seats put between them.

Then with the sickening crunch of metal against metal, the Jeep jerked forward. They sprang apart.

"What the hell?" Ben muttered, peering ahead. Then he realized he hadn't put on the brake. While he had been kissing Carly, the Jeep had rolled down a gentle slope and hit a concrete picnic table. It was a good thing, too, because beyond the table was the lake.

Carly put her hand to her mouth. "Oh, my."

Feeling as inept as a sixteen-year-old on his first date, Ben leaned his forehead against the steering wheel.

With a sound that could have been a smothered giggle, Carly said, "And here I thought it was the kiss that was moving me so." She let her laughter bubble over.

Ben joined her. They laughed until he kissed her again. And there was nothing amusing about this kiss. Carly put her arms around Ben, and as a fisherman might reel in a catch, she gathered his kiss to her. The feelings it aroused spun through her. She went with them. Till she ached from the glory of not being afraid.

He was tender, so tender. With a touch that was just light enough, he stroked her cheek. Then his big, work-roughened hands roamed downward, softly so, till he cupped one breast. Through the thin knit of her blouse, her nipple grew hard as his thumb drew tiny, delicate circles around it. His voice was a deep, seductive murmur against her mouth. She didn't know what he said. All she could do was feel. God, how she felt. All damp and shuddery.

Then his lips left hers, and she opened slumberous eyes and protested. He placed a finger against her mouth. Slowly he followed the contours of her lips. "You have a delicious mouth, Miss Savoy."

She grasped the front of his shirt to draw him closer. "Then come here," she teased.

He held her away. "I have a better idea. Let's get the Jeep up the hill." He drew her hand to his mouth. His lips opened against her skin, lingered, and when he looked up at her his voice deepened. "And after that, let's go home."

Without pausing to think what she might be promising, Carly nodded. She wanted to be with this man. She wanted Ben to be the one who broke through the barrier of her fears.

Getting the Jeep up the hill was a minor task, especially since some customers leaving Sam's came out and helped. The fender was bent, and the damage to the picnic table was minimal. That taken care of, Ben and Carly were strolling hand in hand toward the boat when they heard someone calling them. They turned to see Sam hurrying down the dock.

"I'm sorry," she said. "I don't want to bother you, but I don't . . ." Her voice broke.

In the dim light Carly saw the sparkle of tears on the woman's eyelashes. "What is it?" she said, stepping forward to catch her hand.

"Doc's on a bender." The words came out in a rush, leaving Carly with the impression Sam hadn't meant to say them. Once said, however, they were followed by a garbled explanation about Doc's brother dying. "He's upset," Sam continued. "It wouldn't have happened if he wasn't upset. Boss, you know that, don't you? He hasn't done this in a long, long time."

Ben nodded. "What do you want me to do?"

Impatiently Sam brushed at her eyes. "We've still got customers, and the kids are spending the night with some friends. I know where Doc is, but I didn't want to shut down to go and get him. We..." She lifted her head proudly. "We need the money. It's been slow this month."

"Hell," Ben muttered. "Sam, you know a few dollars don't matter to me."

"But they do to me. Could you watch the place so I can bring him home?"

"Where is he?" Ben asked tersely.

"I can get him," Sam insisted. "If you'll just—"

He stood his ground. "You'll stay here. Now where is he?"

Sam swallowed and then named a beer hangout several miles down the road. After asking Carly to wait, Ben started back to the Jeep.

"Go with him," Carly said softly to Sam. "Go on. I'll mind the store."

"But you don't—"

"I doubt anyone wants more than coffee and a sandwich or a bowl of soup this time of night, and I can handle that. Now go."

Without hesitation, Sam ran after Ben.

They were gone for more than an hour. If there had been a few more customers, Carly might not have watched the clock so closely. As it was, time crawled. Because she was listening, she heard when Ben and Sam got Doc up the stairs to the second-floor apartment. Then she didn't hear anything for a while. The place was cleared and she was flipping over the Closed sign on the door when Ben came in from the kitchen.

"Everything okay?" she asked, crossing to the counter.

Ben shrugged as he slipped onto a stool. "We got him into bed. I decided his wife could take it from there." He propped his head on one hand and idly twirled a saltshaker with the other.

Carly went behind the counter and filled two mugs from the pot of coffee she had just brewed. "Here. You look as though you could use this. Think I should take some upstairs?"

"No. He's dead to the world."

"But Sam . . ."

"Probably won't need anything to help her stay awake," Ben muttered.

She sipped her coffee in silence, watching his tense expression. "Sam said this doesn't happen often," she said finally.

"It doesn't."

"Then why are you so angry?"

Eyes downcast, he rubbed his beard. "Maybe I'm not too thrilled with what I saw from my gender tonight. First Diana's ex. And now Doc. Not much to admire about us, is there?"

"Us? Why are you lumping yourself in with them?"

He shrugged again. "I guess I see myself in what they've done, how they've let others down."

Who had he disappointed? Angela? Carly wanted to ask, but his disheartened attitude prevented her. "I don't think you're like them," she said as she came around the counter and stood in front of Ben. He turned, his bare legs sprawling out on either side of hers. "A guy like them wouldn't have gone running after Doc tonight."

"That was nothing."

She gestured to the room. "The same as making sure Sam and Doc and their kids have a livelihood is nothing?"

He looked at her in surprise. "What do you mean?"

"Remember the first day we came here? I said I thought you were a nice man. That was because Sam had told me the reason you bought this place."

"I had money to invest. This was for sale."

"Oh, sure." Carly darted a glance around the small restaurant. "Don't tell me you're raking in the dough."

"That's not the point."

"Of course not. The point is to give a family that deserves a break a place to live and work. The former owner didn't care much about that, did he?"

"It was a matter of economics. He had to sell."

"And Doc and Sam couldn't buy. Until you stepped in, the only people making an offer weren't prepared to keep them on. You were."

Ben raked a hand through his hair. "Don't go making me out as a saint, Carly. I've gotten plenty from owning this place. It does turn a profit, and I've spent hours and hours doing the things I enjoy."

"Okay, go ahead. Tell yourself that." She grinned. "But I'll believe what I want to believe, the same as Sam does. She thinks you're pretty terrific, you know. Even though she doesn't feel as if she really knows you."

"She knows me...."

"Oh, yes. As well as you want her to know you. You're good at controlling what people learn about you."

Their gazes met and clung. Ben's was the first to fall. "I'm sorry," he offered. "If you expect me to open up, Carly, I just..." With eyes as gray as a stormy sea, he looked at her again.

She stepped closer, till her hips were framed by his parted legs. With gentle fingers she stroked his beard-roughened cheek. "It's okay," she whispered. "I think I know all the really important things about you."

His hand captured hers. "You might be surprised."

"But never disappointed."

"That might be the biggest shock of all."

Stubbornly she shook her head. "I'm not worried."

The smallest of grins touched his lips. "You're pretty sure of yourself, aren't you, Miss Savoy?"

"No. But I used to be. I will be again. I'm relearning some things. Like trusting what I feel right here."

Smiling, she brought their joined hands to her chest, right above her heart.

"Oh, yeah?" His fingers opened, flattened against her. "And what do you feel?"

The warmth of his hand penetrated her skin. She swayed toward him. "I feel like this," she murmured before placing her lips against his.

Given their thin summer clothing and that she was pressed so intimately between his spread legs, it was impossible not to know how he reacted to her nearness. She was glad she excited him. Her own excitement grew until she twined her arms around his neck, drawing him closer, obeying some long-suppressed demand to push her hips against him.

His breathing was ragged as he pulled away. There was something she could only describe as wonder in his eyes as he brushed her hair from her face. "Didn't we leave off at this point once before?"

"I think this is the reason we were headed to the boat."

"Before yet another domestic problem detained us. Funny thing, but I've been wanting to be alone with you all day."

"And people keep getting in the way."

Catching her hand in his, he stood. "Come on, let's make sure everything's in order in here." His kiss was short, hard and full of promise. "Then let's get out before someone else needs us."

They turned off the grill, checked the doors and headed out. Only a last, lingering sense of responsibility made Carly pause on the dock and look back at the building. In one of the lighted second-story windows a shadow fell across the pulled shade. It was probably Sam, pacing the floor. "Are you sure we don't need to stick around? For Sam's sake?"

"She knows what to do."

Carly bit her lip. "Then she really is used to this."

Matter-of-factly Ben said, "Doc's an alcoholic. A recovering one. But sometimes—usually when he's had a setback—he loses his battle."

"You knew that when you bought the place?"

Turning around, Ben followed her gaze to the lighted window as the shadow crossed it again. "The first time I met Doc he was falling down, stinking drunk."

"When was that?"

"Six years ago. It was the dead of winter, the middle of the night, and he was sitting out here on the dock, nursing a bottle of bourbon. The owner of this place had just told him he was selling. It threw Doc for quite a loop."

"He doesn't handle crises very well, does he?"

"Sam's the grounded one. She anchors him. Or holds him up. However you want to look at it."

"She could just walk away. It might teach him to stand on his own two feet."

"And if he fell all the way to the bottom?" Ben demanded, his tone harsh. "How would Sam live with that? How does anyone?" He turned abruptly and headed for the boat.

How do you live with it? The question hovered on the tip of Carly's tongue as she followed Ben down the dock. Whether he realized it or not, he had just re-vealed what she hadn't dared ask about his wife. He still felt responsible for her.

Even though she was dead.

Sitting in the seat beside Ben as his boat skimmed across the darkened water, Carly could feel Angela's presence. She had no idea what the woman looked like, but she saw her. Ben thought of her as his wife. He felt he was to blame for her death.

And for all Carly knew, maybe he was.

The idea was like a wall she couldn't get through. It blocked everything, including the passion Ben had aroused so easily earlier. She eluded his touch on the climb up the path to his house. And standing in the darkened stillness of his beautiful, empty home, she shivered. What was she doing here with this man about whom she knew so little?

Then Ben touched her. And her doubts fled.

He stood behind her, hands on her shoulders, breath warm against her neck. "Please don't be afraid," he whispered.

She turned in his arms. "I'm more frightened of myself than of you."

In answer, he kissed her. He took whatever doubts might have lingered with his lips.

The demands of Ben's body urged him to take her swiftly. He wanted nothing more than to feel her be-neath him, to watch her face as she went a little wild. The urgency of her voice and the hands she pushed over him told him how much she wanted him. Yet he knew instinctively that they had to go slowly. If she trusted him enough to get to this point, he couldn't betray that confidence.

Somehow they made their way to the loft. Ben wasn't sure how long he had fantasized about making love to Carly there. Maybe from the first day they had met. Before they had done more than kiss, he knew the reality would far outstrip his dreams.

They knelt together on the cushions he pulled from the couch. The moon peeped through the skylight and the bank of windows to silver them with fragile light. Her gaze never wavering from his face, Carly tugged her shirt over her head. As quickly as it appeared, the moonlight was gone. She wore no bra, and Ben was left with only an impression of small, pink-tipped breasts and creamy skin. Then Carly's hands were reaching for the buttons on his shirt, and he decided the darkness might be best. If she saw his face, he might reveal everything she made him feel. And there were some emotions he still needed to keep to himself. To hide.

There was no hiding from Carly's touch, however. Her fingers slipped over him. Through the hair that furred his chest. Downward. To the partially unzipped shorts. Beneath them. He caught his breath at her bold, insistent touch.

"No," he murmured. "Baby, I don't need any encouragement."

"But I want—"

He silenced her with a kiss, while his hands pushed her shorts and panties down and out of the way. He pressed her back against the cushions with smooth movements. Naked, she felt small, her bones fragile, her skin sleek. Her scent was like the outdoors. Like the water and the pines and the sun. The combination made him tremble. He was so hard, too hard to last in the way he needed to last for this first time with Carly.

Holding her hands still against his chest, he muttered, "Wait a minute. Please, baby. Wait."

He wasn't sure how long they lay there. It was long enough for him to regain control of himself. Holding her, he allowed the sharpest edge of his need to wane.

Carly stirred restlessly in his arms. "What is it?"

"I want you too much."

She laughed softly. "Is that so bad?" Her hands once again feathered down across his stomach.

He caught them again. "Let it be the way I want it this time. Okay?"

"But, Ben—"

Her protest ended in a choked cry as his mouth moved over one breast. His tongue licked at the nipple, circling, teasing. She arched her back and thrust her hands through his hair as she held him against her.

While his mouth nuzzled her breasts, his fingers did a dance of their own. Across her stomach. Down the satin skin of her inner thighs. Perspiration broke out over her skin. A low moan was torn from deep in her throat.

Fearing she would explode if she didn't touch him, Carly pushed at the shorts that now rode low on his hips. She urged them lower. He kicked them away. His buttocks were firm against her palms. Firm and male. She pulled him against her hip and turned in his arms until they faced each other. Velvet-tipped but rigid, his sex nudged at the juncture of her thighs. She thrust forward, but Ben was having none of that.

Firmly, gently, with kisses and soft, barely coherent words, he eased her onto her back again. And his mouth was on her skin once more. His kisses went everywhere. On her lips. Against the pulse that beat so madly at her throat. Across the scar he couldn't see. Even where her need throbbed with urgent, moist desire. It was with his mouth that he made Carly lose touch with reality.

She was parched.

And Ben was the rain.

Thank God for the rain.

Sometime after that near-delirium, Carly must have slept. For it seemed a long while later that she roused herself enough to realize Ben had pulled an afghan over them. His body was curled around hers. His breathing had settled into an even rhythm.

He was sleeping. Smiling, she turned to study his dimly highlighted features. For a man who had wanted her "too much," he had set aside his own needs. And he had helped her rediscover that part of herself she had thought was lost.

I wasn't afraid.

That wondrous thought tumbled over and over in her head. With Ben she had proven what she had always known deep inside. The rape hadn't really robbed her of anything. Savoring that knowledge, she once again settled against Ben's side.

When she woke again, it was morning. Ben was still asleep. Deeply so. He had moved away from her during the night. Now he lay with only his hips covered by the afghan. His long, muscular legs were sprawled across the carpeted floor. One arm was thrown over his head. He moved restlessly and murmured something as she sat up, but he didn't wake. Picking up his discarded shirt, she stood and slipped it on. Silently she padded downstairs to the bathroom. When she returned, Ben still wasn't awake.

With her back against the edge of the couch, she curled up near him. She sat silent and still for a long time, filling herself with the sight of Ben, waiting for those absurdly thick lashes of his to lift. By the time they did, she had made a decision.

He smiled, and nervously she fiddled with a button on his shirt. "Ben, I have something I want to tell you."

Ben pushed himself up, blinking.

"It's about me," she continued, though the words were hard to force around the lump in her throat. "About when I was raped."

Chapter Seven

Ben already knew what Carly was trying to tell him. As he had told Diana more than two weeks ago, he was aware something had happened to Carly. Since then, he had wondered if it had been rape. Speculating about it had enraged him. The confirmation Carly now gave him brought a sharper, harder anger.

Rape. The word was used every night on the news. It had been dissected, debated and discussed in a wealth of books and movies. Judging by the number of times it cropped up as a topic, the talk shows considered it a popular subject. At this moment, as he watched Carly struggle to tell him how it had happened to her, Ben wished he hadn't changed the channel every time the word was mentioned.

The crazy thing was how beautiful she looked as she prepared to tell him her darkest, deepest secret. The morning sun was in her tangled hair, turning its red-gold highlights to fire. Her eyes were wide and brown. And in his shirt, which hung off her slender shoulders, she seemed smaller. Fragile. Easily hurt.

A new and rawer surge of anger cut through him. Someone had hurt her, brutalized her. Carly. *His* Carly. This wasn't some anonymous stranger on the tube. This was the woman who had made him feel alive again. God, how could anyone have hurt her?

Instinctively he knew his anger wouldn't make the telling any easier for her. And she had to tell him. He could see that in her eyes, hear it in her voice as for the third time she started and failed to begin.

He held out his hand to her. "Come here."

She came into his arms without hesitation. With the afghan tucked around his hips, he leaned his back against the sofa and cradled her close. "Take your time," he whispered into her soft hair. "We've got as long as it takes."

"It might take longer than you expect. Talking about this isn't easy for me."

"You don't have to tell me."

"Yes, I do." Her fingers dug into his upper arm, and she turned her face into his chest.

He felt her ragged, indrawn breath as if it were his own. He couldn't bear to feel her struggling so. "Listen to me, Carly. Knowing about this won't make me feel any differently about you, about last night, about tomorrow."

"I just wish it weren't all so predictable."

He frowned. "What do you mean?"

She turned in his arms, facing him, and her voice became almost flippant. "Oh, you know, high-school principal gets raped. She tried to go on. Can't function. Breaks down. Jumps when a man touches her—"

"Carly, don't—"

She sat up, thrusting her hair from her face. "Dammit, Ben, I was supposed to be strong enough to handle this kind of garbage."

With a hand under her chin, he made her look at him again. "What are you talking about?"

"I'm saying it was stupid of me to fall apart."

"Stupid?" He muttered an oath. "The only thing stupid about what you're telling me is that you're even worried about falling apart."

"You don't understand." She pressed fingers to her mouth and swallowed. "After it happened, I was okay. I didn't think about it. I mean, I even picked the guys—"

"Guys?" Ben repeated, her words only partially sinking in. "Guys?"

Very solemnly she nodded. "Guys. Plural. I picked them all out of a lineup."

Guys. Plural. The emotionless way she said the words made them that much more devastating to Ben. They hurt so much he couldn't bear to look at her. The only thing he could do was hold her even tighter to his side. As if that could erase the horror she had known.

As if anything he could ever do would make it all right again.

He had never known an anger like this. Not when his mother died a senseless death on a California highway. Not when Angela betrayed him. This fury seemed to have its own life inside him. Like a fire-breathing monster, it licked at his insides, consuming him. It was a senseless anger because he could direct it at no one. And somehow, for Carly's sake, he had to contain the feeling. At least until she finished telling him what had happened.

Her work had led her into trouble. Ben thought he could have predicted that. She was passionate about what she did. The few times they had discussed the projects she had set up in her school and its community, he had seen how desperately she cared. And as he knew only too well, passion allows little room for caution. Nearly a year and a half ago, Carly had been working with a student who said he wanted out of the gang he belonged to. Izzy was the name everyone called him. He was bright, Carly said. If he worked hard, he could be more than a dealer or a street fighter. But getting out wasn't easy.

"You can't imagine the pressures on these kids," she whispered. "To stay out of a gang is hard enough. To leave one, well, that's just not done. Sometimes they'd kill you rather than let you go. But Izzy wanted out. And I wanted to help him." She bit her lips and shook her head.

Ben gripped her hand as she told him about the final day Izzy had come to her office. He was agitated.

He said he was tired of senseless deaths. He wanted to do what was right. So he told Carly about the party a rival gang had planned for that evening. Members of his gang were planning a surprise for it. Izzy had made up his mind he wasn't going to help—he knew he'd pay a price for that. He wanted to do more. Carly sent the boy across town to a home for youths run by a priest. Then she called the police.

Her laugh was bitter. "Fewer people would have died if I had kept my mouth shut. That's the damnable part of the whole affair. If I hadn't gotten involved, it would have been just another drive-by shooting."

"But you had to do something."

The look in her eyes was bleak. "Oh, yes, and my efforts were so amply rewarded."

In his struggle to hide his rage, Ben's voice shook. "They came after you, didn't they?"

"Not right away. Not until they figured out Izzy was the snitch."

"Why didn't Izzy lie low?"

She shrugged. "He had a family, Ben. The gang was putting pressure on his little brother, trying to find out where Izzy was. I guess he decided it was better to face the music himself." The muscles in her throat worked as her jaw squared. "God knows how he suffered before he told them about me."

"Then they killed him?"

Pleating the afghan in her hands, she nodded. "Trust me. You don't want the details."

"But didn't you get police protection?"

"By the time they found Izzy's body, I was in the hospital."

"Oh, God." Ben closed his eyes in an attempt to block out the images her words conjured.

"They meant to kill me," she said. "I don't think rape was on their minds when they caught me alone at the school. But one of them thought it sounded like a good idea." Like a child reciting a horror story, she kept on, "I can still hear his voice. Sometimes at home, when I was alone and it was dark, I could hear what he said. Over and over, he said . . ."

Ben stopped her recital by pressing her face to his chest. He didn't want to know what they had said to her. Most of all, he wanted Carly to stop remembering.

But she wasn't through. "I guess in a way he saved my life," she continued, pulling away from Ben. "Because there wasn't time to kill me in the end. One of the cleaning crew came in early that night. They heard him, panicked and ran off." She paused and drew a deep breath. "There have been times when I wished they had killed me instead."

"No," Ben whispered fiercely.

"At least that way it would have been over. Done with."

"But it is over. It's finished."

She pulled back, her eyes searching his face. "That's what I thought at first, Ben. I thought that when my body healed, when those boys were punished, I thought then it would be over."

"So they came after you again."

"No." She sighed. "I guess they thought they'd hurt me enough. For whatever reason, the threats stopped even before the trial. But that's when it got worse for me."

"Worse?" What could be more horrible than what she'd been through?

"Sometimes I couldn't breathe. I'd be walking down a street, and the fear would overcome me. Every stranger's face would be threatening. I couldn't talk to anyone about the way I felt. There were days I couldn't move. I would lie in bed with my heart pounding so, I couldn't hear anything else. On the good days I went back to school. I went back to my job. But there was something strange about the way everyone looked at me, about the way I *perceived* them looking at me."

"You got help, didn't you?"

"Of course. And the things the counselor told me made sense. But it didn't erase the terror, Ben. I couldn't feel safe. That's why I came here this summer. To heal." Fingers threading through her hair, she placed her hands on either side of her head, pushing inward. "I had to try and put myself back together again. Believe it or not, I used to be a fairly sane person."

He touched her cheek. "I believe it. You're sane now."

As Carly looked into Ben's steady gray eyes, something loosened inside her. Perhaps it was the last of the pain that had been born on that long-ago December night. Perhaps she would have let it go without Ben.

But Ben was here. With his calm acceptance. With sympathy instead of pity. "Thank you," she said softly.

"For listening?"

"For not looking at me like I'm a pariah. For not hating me."

His brows drew together in a frown. "Why should anyone hate you? You didn't do anything wrong."

"Oh, I know that." She tapped her forehead. "Up here, I've known that all along. I can't tell you the hours I've sat repeating to myself that I didn't deserve what happened, that it had nothing to do with who I am, with myself as a person. As a woman."

"And it doesn't."

"Of course not," she said fiercely. "But when you live with fear, when you face yourself in the darkest, most silent hours of the night, your mind does funny things. And you start believing things you never ever would have believed before."

His hand went back to her hair, across her cheek, till his knuckles brushed lightly across her mouth. His voice was harsh. "I know, Carly. Believe me. I know what can happen during those dark, lonely nights."

She hadn't cried until then. Strangely enough, the tears hadn't come as she'd talked. But seeing the pain on Ben's face made her eyes fill and overflow. "I know you understand me. Even though I never really believed anyone else did, I know you do. It's crazy, but somewhere, down deep inside, I've known that since the first time we met. But I wish you didn't understand, Ben. I don't like knowing that you've been hurt.''

With gentle strokes he wiped the tears from her cheeks. A smile touched his lips. ''Stefan always told me hurting was just the flip side of happiness. Both are necessary in life.''

Carly forced a laugh past her tears. ''I knew I didn't trust that man. I bet that line came from a movie.''

''Probably. He lives his life as if it was the greatest role ever written. Equal parts tragedy and adventure.''

''And what about you?'' she asked quickly, before she could think about whether he would answer. ''What's your life, Ben?''

The question seemed to shatter the fragile bond that had developed between them. He started withdrawing. Though his body was still close, his gaze darted away from her. ''I am what you see, Carly, just what you see.''

Rising to her knees, she framed his face with her hands. ''No, Ben. There's more to you than that. You won't tell me what it is, but—''

''Carly—''

''Hush.'' She laid her fingers across his lips. ''Don't deny anything. You can choose not to tell me. God knows, I understand how hard it is to talk about some things. But don't tell me lies. Let there be secrets between us, but no lies.''

He started to speak, stopped and drew a ragged sigh. There was regret in the twist of his mouth.

"It's okay," she whispered. "Just as you told me, I don't need to know everything." Even as she said them, Carly wondered if she would regret the words. Secrets fester. The things not talked about were those that exploded in your face. Especially since she cared so much about this man who kept so much hidden.

But she couldn't think about that now. Not when she was so calm. So at peace. Lovingly, her gaze traveled over Ben's face. The deep gray eyes. The strong brows. The thick beard that covered what she knew instinctively was a square, determined jaw. It was a handsome face, one that she still knew she had seen before this summer. Maybe in her dreams? The fanciful thought made her smile.

Ben pulled her down to him, so that she lay across his lap. He cupped her cheek, grinning. "When you smile like that . . ." His voice trailed away as he shook his head. "I wish I had the words for the way your smile makes me feel."

"So you're not a poet, Mr. Jamison?"

He laughed. "I thought I was, hundreds of years ago when I was about fourteen."

She tipped her head back, trying to imagine him younger, his features softer, the beard gone. "Would I have liked you when you were fourteen?"

There was something infinitely sad in his smile. "Most girls did."

"Conceited, aren't you?"

"Terribly so." Still laughing, he leaned down and kissed her.

. It was a simple, direct kiss. It shouldn't have made passion crash through Carly. But it did. Her body turned to liquid and fire as her mouth opened beneath his. His tongue met hers. Sweetly, they twined, tasted. With a rhythm that mocked more intimate acts, he invaded her mouth. Till she whimpered and turned in his arms. Her legs straddled his hips. Her torso strained against his.

Ben pulled away. "You taste like honey," he whispered. He kissed her again, hard and fast, then flashed a wicked grin. "You taste sweet. Everywhere."

Carly flushed, thinking of last night and the way he had loved her with his hands and his mouth. How shamelessly she had moved against him. How moist and warm she grew at the memory of his touch.

Hands moving in slow patterns on her back, Ben chuckled. "I like it when you turn pink like that." She turned her face. He cupped her chin, his voice slipping seductively lower. "Ah, now, don't be embarrassed, Carly. You never have to feel that way with me. Whatever you feel, whatever you do, all of it's fine with me."

Embarrassed wasn't the word for the feelings that were streaming through her. Instinctively she nudged her hips closer to his. She put her hands on his shoulders. How smooth his skin was here. Smooth and brown. Her hands slipped up the strong column of his neck. Leaning forward, she pressed her lips to his throat.

Huskily she said, "My, but your pulse is racing, Mr. Jamison."

"I wonder why?"

With tongue lightly grazing his skin, her mouth moved across his shoulder. His breath caught, and now it was his hips that rotated upward, pressing against the afghan that separated them. His hands went to the buttons on the front of her shirt, but Carly swatted them away.

"You played it all your way last night. Now you pay." Giggling, she drew back, bent her head and captured one flat male nipple with her mouth. Gently she closed her teeth on the puckering bit of flesh. Ben groaned. She sucked harder, and he dragged her head back up to his, kissing her with unrestrained hunger.

She answered him with a need of her own. Hands flat against his hair-whorled chest, she opened her mouth against his, accepting his tongue with greed and want. Excitement curled through her belly. Her nipples became so hard and tight that they hurt. Still kissing him, she tugged at her shirt, trying to undo the buttons.

Ben tore his mouth from hers and took over the task. After what seemed like an eternity of struggling, the shirt was opened halfway and thrust off her shoulders, catching just below her small, sweetly rounded breasts. She arched her back, rubbing her nipples against his chest. With need squeezing the air from his chest, he drew away.

Head thrown back and her body straining against his, Carly was a wanton sight. Already hard, his sex pulsed as his gaze lingered on her breasts. Her nipples were small and pink, just as they'd been in last night's moonlight. This morning they were hard and erect, demanding his attention. At the first touch of his mouth, Carly jerked against him. She groaned, pushing at his shoulder with one hand even as her other held him to her. He bathed her breasts with kisses. Deep suckles. Tiny nibbles. Until she bucked and writhed in his arms.

He moved his lips to the valley between her breasts. "You make me crazy," he whispered against her skin. "Crazy and hot and hard. Are you hot?"

She didn't answer, and with fingers tangling in the hair at her nape, he held her away from him. Eyes half-closed, she was flushed. Her lips trembled.

"Tell me," he repeated. "Are you wild for me?" She nodded. "Then say it."

She swallowed. Her eyes opened, and with obvious effort, she answered, "I'm wild for you, Ben...so w-wild...unbearably hot."

Those breathy words coming from her sweet mouth made him even harder. If that was possible. Ben didn't know if he could grow any harder. His lips caught hers again, and he began easing her backward onto the cushions on which they had slept. Between kisses, he whispered of the things they were going to do to each other. *For* each other. *With* each other. He could feel her shaking, her teeth almost chattering with frenzied excitement. He wanted to feel her—all of her—lying against him. There was too much still separating them. With a curse he sat up and pulled the afghan away. Carly smiled at him. The gesture seemed easy and natural. Welcoming. Yet he paused, struck by the way she looked, sprawled so gracefully across the cushions.

She still wore his shirt. It was bunched up above her slender, tanned legs. The sleeves were halfway down her arms, exposing her lightly freckled shoulders and creamy breasts. The shirt's hem just skimmed the triangle of red-gold curls that bridged her thighs. Leaning forward, he pressed a kiss to those curls.

"Come here," Carly murmured. "Please."

He grinned up at her. "I'll get there in my own sweet time, lady. In my own sweet way." Slowly he undid the bottom button of the shirt, intending to kiss his way up her stomach.

And then he saw the scar.

It wasn't ugly. Pink and slightly puckered, it was a rather neat, thin line. A diagonal slash. He didn't care to think about the sharpness of the blade that had made this cut. Sharp and quick, too, no doubt. It marred the perfect skin of Carly's slender body. A coward's signature.

He sat back. Struggling with the confines of his shirt, Carly pushed herself up. Protectively she gathered the material against her. "I should have told you they did that," she murmured. "I'm sorry—"

"Sorry?" The word felt as if it had been ripped from him. "You're sorry?" Moving quickly, he had her back in his arms. "Oh, sweet Jesus, Carly, you have nothing to apologize for. You don't apologize to me. What those bastards did..." His throat closed. He tried again. "What they did..." He had no words. So instead, he kissed her again.

At once hungry and tender, his kiss made Carly forget the scar, forget those who had caused it. She forgot everything but how much she wanted Ben. How much she needed him.

He brought them back to the cushions. With something akin to reverence, he unbuttoned the shirt and tossed it away. Slowly, softly, he traced the scar with his lips. With kisses so gentle, so slight. As though his touch could make it disappear.

There were tears in his eyes when his mouth reached her own.

She pushed trembling hands through his dark hair, holding him away. "Don't cry for me, Ben."

"I want to take it away," he whispered. "All the pain. All the agony they caused you. I want to take it all." He kissed her. "Give me the pain, Carly. I can stand it. I've stood worse."

She smiled, touching his cheek. "That's why I only want to give you joy."

And she did.

As her hands glided over his body, Ben wondered how he had lived these last, lonely years without her touch. Like a prisoner without a window, he had shut himself off from the world, from the kind of genuine feelings he was sure he didn't deserve. He didn't deserve them now, of course, but Carly didn't know that. She didn't let him accept the limitations he had once placed on himself. She demanded all he had to give. Gladly, he gave.

With a touch that was sure and steady, he took her upward. With kisses and whispers and urgent strokes, they brought each other to a place he had only imagined visiting before. Carly's shuddering body told him she had crested. Then he slipped into her warm, welcoming depths, and she climbed with him again. His release blasted the doors off his prison.

And in that moment, it was all Ben could do to hide the truth from Carly.

He loved her.

How could that be? he wondered when his body had returned to something resembling normalcy. Still joined with Carly, he drew her with him as he rolled to his side. He lay listening as the sound of her breathing evened. God, he loved her. But he wasn't supposed to love. Long ago he had loved, and instead of happiness, he had caused nothing but pain. In his experience, love meant pain and anguish and despair. He couldn't do that to Carly. He *wouldn't* do that to Carly. But how?

It was too late to walk away, to think of taking a step back in their relationship. He had only to look into her gentle brown eyes to know how devastating that would be for her. To get to the point where they were now had taken all of Carly's strength and courage. Beyond that, there was a tiny, selfish part of him that didn't want to step back. He wanted what they had at this moment. The passion. The feeling—even if it was an illusion—of closeness. Dear God, how he wanted her. Just thinking of how they had loved made his body stir again.

Holding her in his arms made him reckless. He knew the dangers, but he couldn't stop to think of where his temerity had taken him before.

Not while Carly smiled at him.

Not when she still sheathed him with such silken heat.

"So hot." As if she'd read his mind she whispered the words, and like a randy teenager, he pulsed inside her again.

Her eyes widened. Then with a sigh of satisfaction, she curved her leg over his hip, angling that softest, most secret part of herself so that she could meet his thrust. A little awkward. Unbearably erotic. The thought of how they were lying, as much as her accommodating body, made Ben grow all the more rigid.

Her arms went around him. His face pressed into the fragrant skin of her neck. He opened his mouth against that tiny spot where her heart beat in such frantic, telling cadence. With one hand on the yielding flesh of her derriere, he held her tight against him. Hips lifting, he drove into her. Once. Twice. Harder. Faster. Till her gasps of pleasure matched the rhythm of his penetration.

For Carly it was a mindless, limitless swirl of pleasure. There was only Ben and the unceasing thrust of his body into hers. He made the seconds slow. They stopped. He twisted the pleasure into a hard, multi-colored ball. Then he spun it outward. And the colors flew in every direction. At the center there was still Ben. Ben and the sound of her own voice, calling his name over and over and over.

Gradually the vortex settled, and he relaxed into sleep. For a long time Carly lay unable to rest, studying the shadows on the wall. She had lived her life in shadows for so long that the happiness she felt seemed somehow too much. She waited, breath held, for the dream to explode like a dam when faced by a flood-swollen river.

The shadows moved.

Ben stirred at her side.

And somehow, the dream held. When she awoke in the early afternoon Ben was still there. Her happiness was, too.

Thank God, the dream held.

They spent the day dozing and making love, finally rousing themselves at sundown to take a shower and search out something to eat. They dulled the edges of their hunger with crackers and cheese while Ben made spaghetti sauce for dinner. Using fresh tomatoes and an array of spices, he ground and measured and mixed, asking Carly to taste everything.

She sat on a stool in his streamlined white-and-burgundy kitchen, trying to decide why she found him so sexy in the white chef's apron he said belonged to Stefan. Perhaps it was because he wore only an abbreviated pair of white shorts beneath that apron. Or maybe it was the way he looked at her as he worked.

His smile was part satisfied male, part teasing child. He turned everything into a sexual game. Sharing kisses in between taste tests. Licking a spoon with a devilish gleam in his eye. Carly assured him there was no way she could make love again—at least for an hour or two. Yet as the sauce bubbled its spicy aroma into the air, they cuddled in the chaise longue on the screened porch. Touches and sighs and kisses. These were a lover's prerogative. Ben used them all, coaxed them all from Carly.

Her lover. She repeated those words silently to herself as she stood in the kitchen doorway, watching Ben empty noodles into a pot of boiling water. He had discarded the apron, and the shorts rode low on his lean hips. Above them, his stomach was flat, marked by the line of hair that angled upward into springy curls on his chest. He had a hunk's shoulders, she decided. Broad but not beefy. Strong arms, too. Strong enough to carry her from the shower to the bed as he'd done this afternoon. She shivered, remembering what had happened in his bed.

"Are you cold?"

Ben's question made her jerk guiltily out of her daydream. Steam was curling up from the pot as he lifted the thin noodles.

"I guess the outfit's a little chilly," she lied, glancing down at the new shirt he had given her to wear.

Holding a colander over the sink, he expertly emptied the pot. "What you need is food. If you'll get the bread from the oven we're ready."

They worked together effortlessly, transferring food from the kitchen to the dining room. Then they dined by candlelight, toasting each other and the day with glasses of iced tea.

Ben ladled sauce over his plate of spaghetti. "I'm sorry if you'd prefer wine, but I don't keep it. Stefan's the connoisseur."

"So you don't ever drink?"

His hesitation was slight but noticeable. "I don't care for the way I feel the next morning."

"Well, in moderation—"

"Yes, that's the trick," he cut in. "Moderation."

The way he said it told Carly moderation and not alcohol was his problem. And yes, that fit, she decided. She had known from the first that he was an all-or-nothing sort of man. "You do everything the way you make love, don't you?"

He looked puzzled.

"All out," she explained. "Full throttle."

Grinning as realization struck, he shook his head. Tenderly he touched her cheek. "Today wasn't an ordinary day, Carly."

She turned her mouth into his hand, pressing a kiss in his palm. "Not for me, either."

As their gazes met and held, she thought he was going to say something more. But they merely looked at each other in silence. She wondered what Ben finally saw in her eyes. There was bleakness in his when he looked away, and there were no more electric pauses for the rest of the meal.

Or for the rest of the evening.

After dinner he chose a John Wayne classic Western from the movie collection that lined his shelves. Carly had seen *The Searchers* on the late movie, but she imagined Ben had viewed it dozens of times. He certainly watched it with a different eye, and with his help she began to appreciate the subtle nuances that had been lost on her. Ben pointed out the dramatic use of color, of figures silhouetted against vast Western landscapes, of actors who expressed more with gestures than words. Of particular eloquence to him was the way a door swung open in the beginning of the film, welcoming Wayne's raw, lonely character into the warmth of home and family. At the end, that same door swings shut, locking him out again.

Savagery and beauty. Love and revenge. What had been a simple story of a man's search for a niece kidnapped by Indians grew in scope as Carly watched it with Ben. The movie spoke to her about deep, aching loneliness. And because Ben seemed to identify so much with the film, she thought it said a great deal about him.

Like the character on the screen, she thought he was standing just beyond an open door. How she longed to pull him in. To keep him there. Safe by the fire.

The strength of her feelings shocked Carly. Was it really less than a month ago that she had come back to the cove? So much had changed. And all because of Ben. Did she love him? What a question that was.

She found she couldn't think about it. It was too soon. Things had happened too fast between them. She didn't put labels on her feelings. But she did stay with Ben that night. She woke with him. The first hot, humid days of July sped past as she spent every moment she could with him.

She didn't need to know his secrets.

What happened next didn't matter.

These were the watchwords she repeated on the nights when she awoke, full of questions. Or when Ben got that bleak, closed look in his eyes. At those times she let him be. She longed to help him fight whatever devils tore at him. She thought she knew something about winning. But with Ben, one couldn't push.

All she could do was leave her door open.

It was Ben's decision about whether he crossed the threshold.

Chapter Eight

My, but this must be a pleasant life."

The soft, laughter-filled comment brought Ben awake with a jerk. Blinking, he looked up into Diana's smiling face. It took him a minute to realize he was on the screened porch of Carly's cabin, the coolest spot they had been able to find for a nap on this mid-July Saturday. Beside him in the hammock, Carly groaned and stirred. Evidently they had both fallen so soundly asleep they hadn't heard Diana's boat or her footsteps coming up the path.

"What are you doing here?" Carly said to her sister as Ben climbed out of the hammock and took a seat in a nearby chair.

"Well, I like that." Diana tossed a bundle of papers at Carly. "Here I've made a special trip to bring you your mail, and all you do is growl at me. Next time I'll let it pile up."

Yawning, Carly swung her legs to the porch floor. "I would have been out to get it."

"Really?" As she took a seat in a lawn chair, Diana regarded them with sparkling green eyes. "It seems to me that the two of you have become virtual hermits. J.D. asked me just the other day what I thought you guys did up here all the time."

Ben stretched and grinned. "And what did you tell him?"

"I told him he'd have to ask you or his aunt Carly, of course."

"Oh, great, put it all on us," Carly retorted, throwing a piece of junk mail at her sister. Diana ducked and they all laughed.

Ben took time to savor the easy familial moment. In the past few weeks, there had been many such small pleasant pauses. Diana and her boys seemed to have accepted that he was part of Carly's life. Diana treated him with casual affection. J.D. shadowed him during visits to the lake. Last Saturday, Ben had taken the youngster and his brother, Griff, on a fishing expedition. It was all very normal. And that was heady stuff for a man who had never known the easy give-and-take of brothers and sisters.

Briefly he wondered how he would have turned out if his mother had moved them away from Hollywood. Or if she had married Stefan or someone else and they had settled down in some nice, normal suburb. Surely then he wouldn't have screwed up so royally.

But wishing to change yesterday was like trying to lasso the moon. Ben shook his head to clear away the regrets. He smiled at Diana again. "Where are the kids?"

Her sunny expression darkened momentarily, then her smile reappeared, falsely bright this time. "Don't you remember? Today's 'W' day."

Ben frowned, and Carly explained, "Their father's wedding day."

"Oh. Right." Thoughtfully Ben rubbed his beard. "So old J.D. decided to be a big guy and put in an appearance, did he?"

Sighing, Diana sat back in her chair, crossed her legs and looked beyond Ben toward the lake. "He told me last night that he wasn't going, but when his grandparents came this morning, he was ready." She leveled her glance on Ben. "I think that's thanks to you."

Carly looked up from the envelope she had been opening. "Thanks to Ben?"

"He had a little talk with J.D. last week."

"I didn't say anything special."

"Yes, you did," Diana said softly. "J.D. told me what you said . . . about not growing up with your father around."

Ben frowned. It sounded as if J.D. had gotten the wrong message entirely. "What I told him about was Stefan. I certainly didn't want him getting the impression that all fathers lose interest in their kids."

"Oh, he understood," Diana said. "J.D. told me everything you said about Stefan, about the weekends you spent with him, the places he took you. J.D. called him an almost-father. He said you told him a person doesn't have to live in your house or be married to your mother to be a good dad. That evidently made a real impression on him."

Relieved that he hadn't done anything to inflame an already sensitive situation, Ben stood and slid his feet into his deck shoes. He hadn't thought the talk with the boy was such a big deal. "I hope you don't mind that I talked to him," he told Diana. "But we were fishing, and he asked me if I thought it was okay if he hated his father."

"Hated him?" Carly echoed. Diana looked stricken.

"Oh, he didn't mean it." Ben smiled a little, remembering J.D.'s uncertain, very solemn expression. "But that's why I decided to say something to him."

"And you reached him in a way I haven't been able to," Diana added. "No matter how I feel about Jim remarrying, I want J.D. to love his father. Thank you, Ben, for talking to him."

"It was nothing." Rather embarrassed by the way both Carly and her sister were regarding him, he started toward the doorway. "If you lovely ladies will excuse me, I'm going to get back to those kitchen shelves I was working on when I decided to take this nap."

As he passed, Carly caught his hand tight in her own. "Like I've told you before, Mr. Jamison, you're a nice man.'' He leaned down to kiss her, and as always she lost herself in the touch of his lips. Then they smiled into each other's eyes until Diana's laughter reminded Carly they weren't alone. Looking pleased with himself, Ben disappeared into the cabin.

With an equally smug grin, Diana settled into the chair Ben had vacated. ''So,'' she said as soon as the pounding of a hammer sounded from inside. ''What *do* you guys do up here all the time?''

Carly felt herself flushing.

Her sister's smile deepened. ''That good, huh?''

''He's been...uh...'' Carly cleared her throat. ''He's good for me, I think.''

''Take it from me. Don't think.''

''I don't.'' When Diana directed a puzzled glance her way, she continued, ''What I mean is that I don't allow myself to dwell on anything. If I did...'' She bit her lower lip, not willing to put into words the way Ben confused her.

But Diana didn't let her off the hook so easily. ''So everything's not so great, huh?''

''It's great, as far as it goes.''

''Where do you want it to go?''

How neatly Diana cut to the heart of the matter. If only Carly could answer in such a succinct, tidy way. There was only one thing she was sure of. Even though she had told herself they didn't matter, Ben's secrets were important to her. She tried to ignore them, but she had a hundred questions that needed answers. ''I want to know who he is,'' she told Diana.

Her sister blinked. "Wait a minute. You want to know who Ben is?"

"Where he came from. What brought him here."

"Then ask him."

Carly shook her head. "It's not that easy."

"Then I'll ask him."

"And you'll get the same kind of evasive answers I have."

Diana straightened in her chair. "Carly, you're with this man every day. I take it from the way you just blushed that you're intimate with him. Do you mean to tell me he won't give you any details about his life?"

"He's a very private person."

"But doesn't sleeping with someone give you the right to know something about him? My God, Carly. A person has to use caution these days."

Caution, Carly thought. Hers had been tossed aside on one of those days when Ben had touched her and chased the numbness and the fear away. She wondered if her sister could really understand that kind of intensity, that desperation. Diana had fallen in love and married so very young. No doubt she still saw the dynamics of a male-female relationship as a series of dates, a neat progression toward a natural conclusion.

Her next comment underlined her attitude. "Dear heavens, Carly, I wish you hadn't gotten involved so fast."

"In one way it seems fast. In another, it's like I've known him forever."

"But it's only been about six weeks."

Carly lifted one eyebrow. "My, but you're cautious now. And you were the one who thought I should get involved with Ben. What happened?"

"I thought you'd get to know each other," Diana retorted defensively. "You know, get answers to the normal beginning questions, like where you grew up. Where he used to live. If he was married..."

Not bothering to tell Diana she knew some of those answers, Carly merely smiled. "Is this the official Diana Hastings dating questionnaire? How do the men you go out with reply?"

Diana's mouth tightened. "I don't go out."

"Then you should."

"Don't start on me, Carly. We're talking about you."

"But maybe you're the one with the real problems now."

Dull color flooded Diana's cheeks. She got up and in what could only be described as a flounce, turned to the cabin. "I'm going in to get my swimsuit," she said. "It's hot, and I'd like to go for a swim."

Carly tossed the unopened mail aside and stood. "Good idea. I'll go with you, and we can continue this fascinating discussion about your love life." The furious warning glance sent by her sister only made her laugh.

She laughed easily these days. No matter how many questions she had about Ben, there was no mystery about the way he had changed her life. She felt strong again. Happy. She was once more the Carly Savoy who used to boast about being equal to any challenge. One part of her, the independent part, liked to think she would have arrived at this state of happiness without Ben. But would she feel this good if she didn't have his smiles to look forward to or if she didn't fall asleep in his arms at night?

Being a mature and sensible woman, Carly knew part of her newfound peace came from pure sexual satisfaction. Making love with Ben was always an adventure. He liked variety. In position. In location. Though she had always considered herself inventive, Ben was more so. They were good together.

And not just in bed. They liked so many of the same things. Good food. Springsteen's early lyrics. Cagney's films. Conversations about the state of the world. Some friendly debate. The soul's sometimes compelling need for silence. Carly could imagine snowy Sundays with Ben in her apartment in New York. She could smell the rich coffee and taste the bacon-and-cheese omelets they would share. Then they would snuggle up under her favorite down comforter and spread out the papers for a long, quiet read. Ben would...

With a start, Carly realized she was imagining Ben with her in New York. That was a long way from the house across the cove and from his life here. Yet when she tried to imagine the distance between them growing greater, she couldn't. In fact, she couldn't imagine a single day without him.

Dressed in her swimsuit, Diana appeared in the cabin's doorway. "I thought you were going to join me."

Giving her an absent nod, Carly moved past her. She found Ben in the kitchen, frowning at one of the shelves he had volunteered to add to the kitchen's limited storage space. Carly took the length of wood out of his hands and stepped into his arms. "Kiss me," she whispered.

He obliged, then drew away. "Any special reason for this display of affection?"

She shook her head. "I'm just glad you're here."

"I'm not going anywhere, either."

"That's even better." She left him standing in the kitchen with a rather goofy smile on his face. And the resolve to discover all about him deepened inside her.

After Diana left that afternoon, Carly and Ben went to his place. It was another of their quiet evenings. Dinner and a movie. This time around Ben's choice was a newer release rather than a classic. Carly had seen it in New York during the holidays the year before. It was a rather standard buddy film, complete with cops and robbers. She had found it merely interesting. It held Ben spellbound.

Afterward, she drifted off to sleep on the couch and woke to find Ben watching the movie again. In the glow from the screen, his expression was rapt. He didn't notice that she was awake, so she watched him in silence. He devoured every second of the movie, frequently rolling the tape back to watch a scene again and again. He looked…envious. Yes, that was it. His face was full of yearning.

Feeling as if she had stumbled upon the key to a treasure, Carly held herself very still. That Ben might have been involved in the film industry fit, considering Stefan's profession. But in what way? The question teased at her until she once again fell asleep.

When she awoke, it was to the coaxing pressure of Ben's lips. Giving herself over to his urgent, sweet loving, she wondered if what she'd seen in his face might be a dream. The next morning she was even more unsure.

They didn't come back to her cabin until the next afternoon, and they'd finished dinner before Carly remembered the mail she had left in the hammock.

It had been the hottest day of the summer yet. Even the screened porch, normally so cool, was stuffy as Ben sipped a tall glass of tea and swayed in the hammock, watching the sunset. Carly sat at the table and sorted through the bills and advertisements that had been forwarded from New York. At the bottom of the stack was a letter from the friend with whom Carly used to work in a community center's youth program. Though Carly hadn't felt up to much of anything last summer, she had volunteered to work with some youngsters on a one-to-one basis. She had asked her friend to keep her apprised of their progress this year.

It was Carly's stifled groan that brought Ben's gaze around to her. Her face pale and drawn, she was staring down at an opened letter with wide eyes.

He set his tea aside and took the chair next to hers. "What's wrong?"

She shook her head, faltered once and then found her voice. "We . . . they lost one."

"Lost one?"

"A teenager I worked with last summer." Slowly she folded the letter and slid it back into the envelope. "I thought she had kicked her habit for good, but I guess she decided the struggle wasn't worth it."

"So she's back into drugs."

"No." Tucking a strand of hair over her ear, she looked up at Ben with sad eyes. "She's dead."

He let out a long breath. "I'm sorry."

"Sometimes I wonder why I care so much," she murmured.

"You wouldn't be Carly if you didn't care."

"Yes," she agreed. "The eternally optimistic fool."

"Being hard on yourself, aren't you?"

Her only answer was a bitter laugh.

"Come on," he pressed. "You win more than you lose."

She shook her head. "I've never really broken it down, but I think right now I'm losing the war."

Slipping an arm around her shoulders, Ben put his cheek against her hair. "The important thing is that you try. I admire that about you."

"Do you?"

The sharpness of her voice made him blink and pull away. "Why do you sound so surprised?"

Sighing, she tapped the envelope against the table. "I don't know. I guess I'm just questioning the sense in even trying to make a difference. These kids..." She held up her right hand as if trying to make a point and then closed it in a gesture of defeat.

"Tell me about them," Ben pressed.

"Haven't you heard enough of my inner-city horror stories by now?"

"It's what you do. I want to know about it."

Her chin lifted. "It may not be what I do anymore."

"You don't mean that."

She faced him, her expression serious. "How can you sound so sure of what I'm so uncertain about?"

"Because you're a fighter."

"And how do you know that?"

His answer came without thinking. "Someone who gives up easily would have let those bastards who attacked her win."

She gazed at him for a moment before giving in to the smile that tilted the corners of her mouth. "You're right. I am a fighter."

Folding his arms on the table, he leaned forward, shooting her a sideways admiring glance. It pleased him to see Carly looking as she did. So strong and sure of herself. Even a little cocky. Beneath her soft, fragile exterior, she was made of steel. Carly was tough enough to bear a world of burdens.

As he had a hundred times, he compared her to Angela. There were similarities, yes. Like most people, he supposed there were certain qualities he was attracted to in the opposite sex. Carly had Angela's sweetness, her giving nature. But Carly had reserves of strength that Angela had never dreamed of. Perhaps it was that Carly was a woman, while Angela had never progressed very far from being a child. The realization hit Ben like a thunderbolt. Strange how it had taken being with Carly for him to see what Stefan had been saying for years about Angela.

"What is it?" Carly asked when he had stared at her for a long moment.

He shook his head. He didn't want to discuss Angela with her. Angela was in the past. "Tell me about some of the battles you've won," he suggested instead. "I'm sure those are stories you won't mind sharing."

Carly considered for a moment and smiled ruefully. "Well, actually, there are a few kids in my school and at the center who haven't gotten pregnant or joined a gang or started selling drugs."

"See, it's not all bleak."

Her eyes narrowed. "But most of it is, Ben. For so many of them it seems like a hopeless world."

"With no way out?"

"That's it exactly. Some of the bright ones escape by using their heads. Too many get caught in an endless cycle. They have children when they're too young."

"And pass on the burdens."

"Exactly. Their life seems so worthless. At times I can understand why they escape into drugs. I'm sure for some of them it looks like the only escape."

Her words had an all-too-familiar ring to Ben. Body tensing, he sat up. "There's nothing to worry about when you're high."

"And when you're not high . . ."

"Then you worry about getting there again." Perspiration began to gather on the small of his back. His voice faint, he said, "And at least that gives you a goal. A purpose."

She glanced at him, her eyebrows drawing together in a frown. "It's not exactly the way they show it on the news, Ben."

"I know that." *God, the things I know.*

"I mean, it's worse than they could ever show," she insisted, shuddering.

Worse, yes, he knew about worse.

"People will do anything, betray anyone for a little more smack, another rock—"

"Yeah," he whispered. "Anything." He couldn't stop the pictures that went through his head. No matter that he didn't want to dwell on the past, he couldn't help but remember. Especially when the world she was painting was so bitterly familiar. "Carly," he said slowly. "Please, Carly . . ."

But she wasn't listening to him. She was staring hard at some point over his head. "Ben, can you imagine being so lost, so utterly—"

He shoved the table away. Its legs screeched along the floor, and Carly, who had been leaning against the edge, rocked forward, catching herself before she fell. Her gaze shifted in startled amazement to his face. Hands balling into fists, he pushed out of his chair and stalked away.

"Ben—"

"I know," he muttered, turning to face her again. "I know what it feels like, Carly."

She stood and took a tentative step forward. "Ben, I was just—"

"Don't you understand?" He grasped hold of her shoulders and gave her a little shake. "Listen to me, Carly. I know about everything you're telling me. I was doing drugs when you were still playing with dolls."

The horror came to her face, just as he'd known it would. It couldn't get any worse than the look in Carly's sweet, trusting eyes.

She tried to cover it, though. Bless her heart, she tried her damnedest. "My God, Ben, there aren't many people our age who haven't experimented with something or other. It isn't a tragedy or even the end of the world."

He shook her again. "I'm not talking about smoking some dope in your dorm room, Carly."

"Well, neither am I, Ben. I know—"

"You couldn't," he bit out. "You couldn't know unless you've been there." No matter what she'd seen in New York, he'd lay odds he could still shock her. And that's just what he decided to do.

Still holding her by the shoulders, he told her about stealing money from his mother's purse to buy speed when he was twelve. "Speed, Carly. I was stealing from my mother because I wanted a cheap thrill."

"You were young—"

He thrust her away. "You know better than to make excuses for that sort of thing. Would you excuse it in one of your students?"

"Of course not."

"I was a filthy little thief. Like all of those kids you work with, I thought my life was so bad." He laughed without feeling any mirth. "Bad. Can you imagine that? I had a mother who loved me. And Stefan who would have killed for me. And plenty of everything money could buy. But I had an attitude, too. Doing drugs was cool, and at all costs I had to be cool. I was—" He stopped and turned away. Though he had already told Carly more than he'd ever intended, there were some parts of his life he refused to allow her to examine. There were some broken dreams even he couldn't examine. He still felt the loss of part of what he had thrown away.

"No," she said, grasping his arm and forcing him to look at her again. "What were you going to say? What were you?"

He swallowed. "A spoiled little privileged brat," he managed at last. It wasn't the whole truth, but it was all he wanted to say. "Oh, I straightened out for a while. I found something I wanted to do. Something I loved." He swallowed. God, the feeling of doing what he loved best. He would never know that again. "I was high on what I did for a while. I didn't need drugs then. But when everything wasn't going my way..." He shook his head. "Man, I thought the whole world was supposed to revolve around me. And then I fell in love."

The muscles worked in Carly's throat. "With Angela?" she whispered.

If the pain streaking through him weren't so sharp, he would have managed a laugh. "Angela?" he repeated "God, no. I fell in love with cocaine."

Carly took a step backward. His voice steady, devoid of emotion, Ben described himself as she couldn't imagine—a slave to a fine white powder. He had lied for it, stolen for it, betrayed everyone who trusted him. And all for a few moments of flying. What sort of troubles had sent him down that escape hatch? she wondered. It was hard to picture the calm sensible man she had come to know being so obsessed. But he said he had lived from high to high, his days dominated by increasing paranoia. Ceaselessly he had measured and remeasured his supply, trying to make sure he had enough to get him through until the next score.

It wasn't a new story, not nearly the worst story Carly had heard. It shocked her a little, yes, but only because this was Ben who had lived so desperately, destructively. And the way he had told her had been startling, too. The truth had come so suddenly, from out of the blue. But he *had* told her. She couldn't help but celebrate that as a victory.

"So?" he demanded as she continued to look at him.

She lifted her chin. "So what?"

That made him pause.

"What do you want?" she asked, stepping close to him again. "Do you want me to get angry? Are you expecting me to ask you to leave?" Eyes narrowing, she studied the pained look that crossed his face. "Is that it, Ben? Did you hope by telling me this that I'd throw you out? Would that be easier than leaving on your own?"

"God, no." The words sounded as if they had been torn from him. She didn't doubt them.

"Then why act as if I'm supposed to push you away?"

His mouth twisted sarcastically. "Oh, so it doesn't bother you that you're sleeping with an addict."

Such a telling choice of words. Softly, she asked, "Don't you mean *ex*-addict, Ben?"

He shoved a hand through his hair. "Yes, ex—"

"It strikes me as odd how many things about the past you still refer to as if they're part of your life now. There's this." She reached out and took hold of his hand. "And there's Angela, too."

"I told you—"

"That she's dead," Carly cut in. "But you still call her your wife. You still call yourself an addict. How long have you been clean, anyway?"

"A long time."

"How long?" she insisted.

"Ten years."

About as long as he'd said he'd been apart from Angela. Carly had to wonder if the two events were linked. She lifted her gaze to the ceiling and let out a sigh. "I know the temptation is always there for you, Ben. I know it isn't easy, but it sounds to me as if you're winning, and winning big. So why are you still trying to punish yourself for the mistakes you made?"

"It isn't that—"

"Isn't it?" He started to pull away, but she grasped his other hand. "Don't expect me to punish you, either."

"I don't." His voice sounded choked. "That's the last thing I want, Carly. But the things I've done . . ."

Her fingers laced through his. "I certainly didn't expect you to be perfect, Ben. You're a man, not a child. You lived before the day you came strolling up my path. Nobody's perfect."

His hand squeezed hers, and his gray eyes seemed to rake over her face. "You're close," he whispered finally. "Pretty damn close."

"Oh, yes," she murmured, trying to smile. "I'm so perfect. That's why I was jumping at the sound of bugs hitting the window when I arrived here. That's why the office staff at school calls me Carly the Hun when they think I can't hear them. I'm obsessive about things like paper clips and hairpins. I can be incredibly bitchy. I—"

"Okay," Ben interrupted. "So you're only ninety-nine percent perfect. I'll give you that."

With a sigh she stepped into his arms. He hugged her close. "I'm so glad you told me," she murmured against his chest. "I was beginning to think you'd never trust me enough to tell me what you were hiding."

"You trusted me with your secrets."

She tipped her head back. "I'd trust you with my life."

He touched her cheek, his expression filled with something she could only call awe. "I don't know that I deserve that, Carly."

"Of course you do." She lifted her lips to his. Gently they kissed. Then she drew away. "You are the most patient, caring man I have ever known. Look at what you did for Doc and Sam. For J.D. Not to mention me.''

A faint, devilish twinkle chased the pain from his eyes. ''Everything I've done for you has been for selfish reasons.''

Her lips curved upward. ''If what we have together comes from your being selfish, all I've got to say is . . . don't change.''

His fingers traced her features. Carly closed her eyes and let the sensations run through her. First there was Ben's scent. He smelled of soap and something she thought of as merely male. As basic as the earth and the sky. Breathing the fragrance in, she felt a little unsteady, but perhaps that was from the heat.

The night was so hot. So still and humid. Perspiration dampened her scalp as she stood there while Ben touched her face. Her lips parted as his thumb rubbed across them. Once. Twice. Her tongue flicked against his thumb, and she heard him suck in his breath. It felt as if that sound spiraled all the way through her. His hand moved down. She lifted her chin as he skimmed down her neck. Then to her breasts. Her nipples budded at his light, barely perceptible touch. The sensation turned her to honey. She lifted her hands to his shoulders for support.

As if he read her thoughts, Ben cupped her rear in his hands and lifted her up. Their lips met again as her legs went around his hips. He took two steps forward and placed her bottom on the edge of the table. Her legs still clasped him close. She rubbed against the erection that strained his zipper. With strong arms and legs, he half supported her weight, making the strain seem effortless. The thought of the sleek, bunching muscles beneath his T-shirt made Carly damp with need.

"I want you," she muttered against his mouth. With her teeth she nipped at his bottom lip. "I always want you."

His laughter was a growl made deep in his throat. "I'm beginning to think you're insatiable, Miss Savoy."

"Not until you," she answered. "No one has ever consumed me this way."

He pressed his hips forward. "Consumed, huh? It sounds like you're crazy about me."

"About you. For you." She caught his lips with hers again, groaning as his tongue plunged deep into her mouth. She tugged at his damp shirt. "Take this off."

"Getting kind of bossy, aren't you?"

"Carly the Hun, remember?"

"I've always had a problem with dictators." Though his hands slipped to her waist to hold her steady on the table, Ben stepped back. His fingers hooked into the elastic waistband of her brief running shorts. "You first."

She braced her hands behind her, lifted her hips and allowed him to strip away her shorts. He unbuttoned her blouse and unhooked her bra, though he didn't push the cups completely away from her breasts. Her panties he left. "Very nice," he whispered, running his fingers across the triangle of lacy material.

He watched Carly's eyes close again as his hands stroked the smooth, sleek skin of her thighs. Down and then up. Her legs spread a little wider. His thumbs met in the center of the delta between them. He pressed down, and Carly gasped, rotating her hips upward. Her head went back. A trickle of perspiration, caused by the heat or perhaps by her excitement, rolled between her breasts. Ben bent over her, catching the salty moisture with his lips. Drawing away, he slipped one thumb beneath her panties. Unerringly, he found the sensitive but hardening kernel of flesh he sought. He rubbed. Lightly. Then harder. And Carly exploded.

While the climax still shook through her body, he drew the panties down her legs. He paused to push his own clothes out of the way, and then he thrust into the body she offered so willingly.

Carly strained against him, lifting her legs high around his waist. Relentless in pursuit of her own pleasure, she met his every plunge with a parry of her own. And she told him things. She had never dreamed of half what she asked him to do. Amazingly enough, he managed to accomplish all of it.

And when the storm of loving passed, they both slid to the floor and lay there, gasping, covered in perspiration. It was so hot. Carly didn't think she had ever been so miserably hot. At the same time, she had never felt quite so wonderful. Finally Ben stripped all of his clothes away and stood, pulling her with him.

"But I can't move, much less walk," Carly protested.

"Yes, you can. We're going to cool off." He tugged her toward the door, and she stumbled after him down the path, losing her shirt and bra on the way.

They dove from the end of the dock. After a day of being warmed by the July sun, the cove's water should have felt tepid. But against Carly's fevered body it was mercifully cool. Feeling as free of cares as she was of clothes, she stroked effortlessly through the water, arms pumping, heart full to bursting with love for the man who swam by her side.

She didn't question when she had begun calling her feelings for Ben love. She just accepted it, in the same way she had accepted the simple pleasure of moving through the water, the same way she had absorbed Ben's confession about his drug-scarred past. The truth had never frightened Carly. She could deal with whatever lay out in the open.

Only the knowledge that Ben probably still hid something from her gave her pause. But she pushed the unease away. Tonight, there was no room in her heart for doubts.

With the moon and stars providing the only light, Ben thought the mountains hovered closer than usual. The cove seemed smaller. The lamps burning in Carly's cabin and at his house appeared far away. If he closed his eyes, he could imagine they were the only two people in the world. Or on some far distant world. Swimming in some moon-dusted sea.

In that world, he had no reason to doubt the way Carly had reacted to tonight's confession. There, he wouldn't have to worry that the love shining in her eyes would someday change to hurt.

There, Carly would never leave him.

What a pity a world such as that didn't exist.

Regret was already edging aside his joy when he turned to swim toward the dock, back to reality.

Chapter Nine

Carly put the phone's receiver in its cradle and sat staring at it for a moment. Outside this tiny office alcove swirled the spicy scents and busy sounds of Sam's kitchen, reminding her of how far she was from the woman she had just spoken with on the phone. New York City. It was both light-years and hundreds of miles from this pleasant restaurant at the edge of the lake.

"Bad news?" Sam leaned against the archway that divided the alcove from the kitchen, regarding Carly with concern.

"Just my boss," Carly murmured. Sam didn't question her further. That wasn't her way, but Carly felt compelled to explain. "She's wondering if I'll be reporting for work in two weeks."

Turning a page on the wall calendar that hung nearby, Sam sighed. "Hard to believe it's August. The vacation's almost over."

"I suppose." Carly bit her lip, not wanting to think about leaving here.

Sam gave her a long, considering look. "Come on," she said at last. "Let's go upstairs and have a cup of coffee and a piece of pie."

"But you're busy—"

"The kids can handle it for a while." Sam's brilliant smile flashed as she pointed to the kitchen's central work island where several pies covered in brown-peaked white swirls sat waiting. "It's chocolate cream with meringue."

Carly couldn't resist chocolate. "Let's go."

Sam called some instructions to her son and daughter and, with pie in hand, led the way up the stairs to their living quarters. Setting an insulated coffee pitcher down on the round dining table, Carly looked about with interest.

Since the night Doc had tied one on at the local watering hole, Carly and Ben had been coming regularly to the restaurant. Ben, of course, had work to do much of the time. He had run the tackle shop for a few days while Doc went home for his brother's funeral. Carly had taken to slipping into the kitchen to chat with Sam and her kids. When it was busy, she pitched in, dipping bowls of chili, throwing burgers on the grill, chopping vegetables for salads. The initial rapport between the older woman and her had grown into a casual friendship. But this was the first time she had been invited into the family's home.

Though she hadn't given the matter much thought, the apartment looked the way Carly would have imagined Sam and Doc's place to be. The Southwestern influence of their native Texas was seen in the colorful serape that hung on one wall and the vibrant pillows on the worn sofa. Record albums lined the shelves near a stereo system. Beside the dining table was a broad, uncurtained window that overlooked the dock. On the wall in front of Carly, a framed poster extolled the virtues of peace and love.

Sam, who had slipped a vintage Carole King album on the stereo, saw her guest studying the poster and laughed. "What can I tell you? It hung over the bed where Doc and I first made love. I have a sentimental attachment to the thing."

Sitting down, Carly accepted a steaming mug of coffee. Music she hadn't heard in years rolled over her. "Gosh, that sounds good."

"It's one of my favorites. I like to think I'm a with-it kind of mom, and I do my best to listen to what the kids bring home. But when I really want music, I go back about twenty years." She took a seat, shaking her head. "I can't believe it's been that long since this was a hit."

"Ben told me you and Doc were flower children."

"Is that what we were?" Sam cut Carly a thick wedge of pie. "We did grow our hair long and wear bell-bottoms and love beads and little else. And I vaguely remember Doc putting flowers in my hair somewhere in San Francisco.''

''Sounds as if you fit the bill.''

''Yeah, well.'' Flipping her long, dark braid over her shoulder, Sam smiled again. ''At least I've still got the hair. Doc's is going fast. He started losing it about the time we decided we couldn't change the world.''

Carly paused with a fork full of pie halfway to her mouth. ''And when was that?''

''When we had to start buying diapers.'' She grinned. ''I mean, we were living on a farm at the time, and I made my own baby food. It was warm, so the kids didn't need many clothes. I found out with the first one that if you give your baby your breast, lots of love and a pot to bang on, they're pretty content. But you always have to have diapers. And buying them takes money. We sold out in favor of keeping our babies' bottoms dry.''

They laughed comfortably together, but as they ate their pie Carly again darted a glance around the room. She looked out the window at the stunning view of water and mountains and thought of the handsome boy and girl who were working downstairs. ''I don't think you sold out,'' she told Sam. ''Not at all.''

Sam sipped her coffee, giving the room a satisfied glance. ''It's not a bad life, is it? I like what I do. I love my family. Maybe that's all we can ask for.''

''A pragmatic view. And here I had you tagged as a romantic.''

''Because I save posters from my misspent youth?''

"No," Carly said softly. "Because you've stayed with the man in the front room downstairs."

Cocking one eyebrow inquiringly, Sam murmured, "Oh, is that romantic?"

"Well, I know you love him."

"Sure I do, but that's not romance. Cleaning him up after he's been on a three-day drunk doesn't have anything to do with romance. It has a lot to do with love, though. The two are very different."

"Have you ever thought about leaving him?"

"Of course. And if he pulled what he did last month very often, I would leave. But he doesn't. Not now."

"And when he did?"

With finger stroking thoughtfully over her mouth, Sam paused a moment. "I think I spent most of my time feeling responsible for what he was doing to himself. When I let go of that, I was okay. I stopped making excuses for him. He pulled himself together, gave up the drinking for the most part, and we moved here."

Carly felt sure there was more than that to Sam and Doc's story, but she didn't press for details. "He's lucky," she murmured.

"So am I." Dark brown eyes sparkling, Sam poured more coffee in Carly's mug. "But I didn't invite you up here to talk about me and my old man. Why don't you want to go home to New York?"

"Did I say I didn't want to go?"

"After you got off the phone, you looked like a kid on the last day before school starts. I just assumed it was because you didn't want your vacation to end."

Sighing, Carly patted her fork across the crumbs that remained on her plate. "I guess I don't." Briefly she explained that her supervisor had called Diana last week, asking Carly to phone her. School for teachers and staff started a full two weeks before Labor Day, when they gathered for meetings and made plans for the coming year. Usually Carly was eager to get back to her work. This year, she dreaded it. She was even thinking of quitting.

"Don't want to leave Ben?" Sam asked.

So it was that obvious. Elbows on the table, Carly steepled her fingers. "I hate to think of leaving him here all alone."

"He was alone when you came."

"I know..."

"Then don't you mean you hate to go?"

Carly looked up in surprise. "That's what I said."

"No, you said you didn't want to leave him here," Sam said firmly. "That doesn't mean you don't want to go."

"I think it does," Carly insisted. "I just want to be with Ben. I want what we've had this summer."

Settling her chin in her hand, Sam gazed out the window again. "Summers fade."

Carly sent her profile a sharp glance. "What does that mean?"

Her answer was a question. "Would you be willing to stay here?"

"Of course."

"Sure about that?"

A keen edge of irritation cut through Carly. "I said yes, I would. What else do you want?"

Sam shifted in her chair. "Never mind. It's none of my business."

"I'm asking you, aren't I?"

Frowning, Sam said, "Carly, I just don't think you've considered what staying here would mean. Could you really live here with Ben year round?"

"Why not? I have family in Cleveland. God knows, my sister could use my help right now. I could get a job teaching."

"And give up your whole life in New York?"

Taking a deep breath, Carly said, "I was thinking about doing just that before I ever met Ben."

"You'd give up your work? The projects you've told me about?"

At the beginning of the summer, Carly hadn't considered that giving up what she did would bring even a faint pang of remorse. In those last, rotten months in New York, many hours had been given to the fantasy of walking away from her job and never looking back. Even a few weeks ago, after receiving the letter from her friend at the center, she had thought of how lucky she was to be gone. But now, faced with Sam's thoughtful, probing questions, she knew a moment's hesitation. Could she give it up?

"Not as easy as you thought?" Sam asked.

"I guess not. But I still think I'd choose Ben."

"It wouldn't be like this summer."

Carly lifted her chin at that. "I think we could keep it that way."

"Maybe you could," Sam conceded. "But you have to consider what this summer has been about." She drew a deep breath. "Now, I don't pretend to know exactly how things are between you and Ben, but I'd be willing to guess that this has been a special time for you, an interlude, something of a romantic adventure. Am I close?"

Thinking of those nights when she and Ben had swum under the stars, the days when they had made love whenever and wherever the notion struck them, Carly felt her face grow warm.

Sam grinned at her. "I can see I'm right. It's nice to know I haven't completely forgotten what it's like when someone sweeps you off your feet. But staying here with Ben wouldn't be like that. Day in and day out the romantic-adventure stuff can wear pretty thin."

"But I love him," Carly said fiercely. "Doesn't that count?"

"Sure it does." Sam patted her arm. "But I hope you see that continuing to love someone like Ben won't be easy."

"Why do you say that?"

"Because he's deep into himself, sort of like Doc." She shook her head at Carly's surprise. "Yeah, I know, my husband seems like one of Santa's friendlier elves. But that's an act. The real Doc is hidden several layers beneath that. Even I have to work to reach him."

Carly could understand that. Sometimes she felt Ben holding back on her, retreating into himself. Even since telling her about his problems with drugs, he could still be remote. She still didn't know much about Angela. She didn't even know how Ben had earned the money he seemed to have in such abundant supply.

"Think carefully before deciding to stay," Sam said, breaking into Carly's thoughts.

"I don't have much time."

"Just don't give up everything else in your life for him. I mean, maybe Ben's happy in his little lakeside hideaway. You might be miserable."

"It's hard to imagine being miserable with Ben."

Sam chuckled. "You see. Love can cloud your reasoning abilities."

A shout from downstairs indicated Sam's sojourn from her duties had to end, but for the rest of the day Carly couldn't put the conversation out of her mind. It seemed to her that Sam was saying the difference between spending the summer here and staying year round was the difference between romance and love. One was frivolous and exciting. The other was something altogether more serious.

But she did love Ben. He was much more than a summer lover. Yes, he was exciting. And yes, she knew maintaining that same level of excitement was nearly impossible. But if there was a foundation of love, a solid, strong relationship could be built. She could be happy here with him.

If he wanted her to stay.

Strangely enough, Carly hadn't even considered that question. She'd just assumed Ben would be glad if she told him she wanted to stay. What if she was wrong?

And how could they build anything when so much remained a mystery about him?

The early days of August disappeared as Carly rolled the questions around in her mind. On Saturday morning, her doubts drove her from bed at an early hour. She stood at the window in Ben's bedroom while he slept, watching the sun turn the mist on the lake to shrouds of rose and gold. In a week and a half, she might be in New York. The view from her apartment was of other buildings. True, there were a dozen museums only a short ride away. There were art galleries and exhibits and every type of restaurant imaginable. But would they compare with these mountains when the trees flamed red and gold and orange this October?

There was her work, too. Carly considered the times she had "won," as Ben had put it. Who would be there for the students who needed her help? She wasn't indispensable, a fact her principal had been fond of pointing out those times when Carly had argued about paperwork and various other forms of red tape. But who would take her place if she left just like the countless other educators who had fled the system in recent years? It could be someone with enthusiasm and guts. Or it could be someone for whom the position would be a job and nothing more. The thought appalled her, even as she asked herself what it mattered. For she knew nothing would fill the empty places in her heart if she was far from Ben.

She wanted him to say he needed her. She knew he did, of course, but she wanted that message to come from him, to be spelled out. Being needed was essential to Carly's happiness. It was why she had dedicated herself so completely to her work. It was part of every friendship she'd ever had. Perhaps it meant even more to her than love. If Ben said he needed her, then her decisions would be made easy.

She turned from the window to find him sitting up in bed, watching her. Dark hair tousled, sheets pushed to his waist, he presented a sexy sight. It would be so much easier to think coherently about their future if the sight of him didn't leave her so breathless. *Romance,* she told herself, *just romance.* Her voice was steady as she said, "I thought you were still asleep."

"Why aren't you?"

"The morning's too nice to miss."

"I used to never miss the dawn, either," he murmured. His smile was slow. Indescribably appealing. "But that was before my nights became so full."

He drew her like a magnet back to the bed. Slipping under the covers, she cuddled next to him.

"What were you thinking about?" he asked.

Carly seized the first thing that leaped into her head and told him what Sam had said about the reasons she had stuck it out with Doc.

"I guess you'd call it true love," Ben said. "Like I said, Sam's a strong woman. Rare, too. Most people would have left him."

"Did Angela leave you?"

The question startled Ben. He had grown used to Carly's not pushing for details about his life. And though he had told her what was perhaps the worst of it, he wasn't ready to reveal the rest. Avoiding her gaze, he swung his legs out of bed.

But Carly wasn't backing down this time. "Did she leave?"

His back to her, he focused his attention on the painting that hung on the wall across from the bed. The abstract, in shades of blue, was the only thing he had kept from the house he and Angela had shared. Stefan had brought it to him after Angela was dead. Ben could remember the day they had found it. In Carmel. At a little shop where the ocean wind had kept pottery chimes in constant motion. Neither of them had been stoned that day. He had told Angela the painting reminded him of the blue lights in her eyes. They had hung it in the living room, so that it was the first thing he would see when he came in the front door and turned the corner. On that last day, when Angela sank to the bottom, he could remember turning the corner, seeing the painting and then looking down...

Stifling a groan, Ben brushed a hand across his eyes. *No. He never thought about what he had seen that last day with Angela.*

"Ben?" Carly touched him, her hands cool against his shoulders, but he shook her off and stood.

He was at the door to the bathroom when she spoke again. "Why won't you talk about her?"

He didn't turn, but with jaw set, he answered, "I left her, all right. I was the one who walked out of our house. Does that satisfy you?"

"No." The thread of anger in Carly's voice made him turn. She was so rarely angry. She got out of bed and walked toward him. "It doesn't satisfy me, Ben. I don't understand why you can't tell me about what happened with her. Why is everything about you such a big, dark secret?"

"It's not," he lied, cursing himself even as he uttered the placating words. "I just don't like talking about her. Our marriage was a...a mistake. And most of the problems were my fault. The drugs' fault."

"But I understand that—"

His voice rose, came out harsher than he intended. "Carly, you don't . . ." He lifted his hand, then simply grasped the edge of the doorjamb and evened out his voice. "Do we have to talk about this?"

"I want to."

"Well, I don't," he retorted. At Carly's wounded expression, he muttered a curse. "I don't see why it's so important."

"Don't see?" she echoed faintly, falling back a step. Running one hand through her hair, she gestured toward the bed with the other. "Doesn't this give me any rights at all? I mean, other than the obvious ones."

That hurt. He didn't think of Carly as simply his lover. "Of course," he said.

"Then tell me what happened to Angela."

His jaw tightened again. "I've already told you. We got a divorce. Two years later, she killed herself."

"But why did you get the divorce?"

The pictures flashed through his head again. Harsher this time, in more detail. His throat felt as if it were closing up. "Irreconcilable differences," he managed at last.

"Ben, that's no answer."

"Well, it's all you're getting," he bit out. Turning, he grasped the bathroom doorknob and started to swing it closed. Carly blocked the motion with her body. Ben closed his eyes, praying for strength. "Please," he said in as smooth a voice as he could muster. "Please move, Carly."

"Not until you tell me all of it."

"All right, dammit!" he yelled. Carly's eyes widened, and she stepped out of the doorway. Ben followed her, and in his anger he spoke recklessly. "You want all of it? Okay. Then here's her name—Angela Dane. Ring any bells?"

Mutely Carly shook her head.

"How quickly they forget," Ben muttered. "Go to the library and look it up in the newspapers if you want all the gory details, but I understand she blew one too many lines of coke and then blew her brains out in a Vegas hotel." Not pausing to see what effect the announcement had on Carly, he once again stepped into the bathroom. This time he slammed the door behind him.

When he finally came out, Carly was gone.

His first instinct was to go after her. But he resisted, knowing he wasn't in the right state of mind for discussing his relationship with Angela and the way it had ended.

For half the day, he paced the house like a trapped cougar, moving from window to window as he stared across at Carly's. It looked like his little outboard boat bobbing at her dock. The outline of her father's boat was visible in the shadows of the boathouse, too. That meant she probably hadn't taken off for the library yet. Damn, why had he told her Angela's name? The secret would be out whether he told her or not.

He went down to his own dock and headed out in the ski boat, intending to go see her, but midway across the cove, he turned the boat toward the opening that led to the lake. He still couldn't think of talking to Carly. At the restaurant, business was slow. So he hung around, drawing curious looks from Sam and from Doc, who was enjoying a cup of coffee at the counter.

Finally Ben retreated to the relative privacy of the office alcove and called Stefan.

They had talked just last week. In fact Stefan had been in almost constant contact since he'd left in June. With obvious glee, he had followed the progress of Ben and Carly's relationship. Ben had given him a minimum of details. But Stefan had always been able to read him, gaining as much from what Ben didn't say as what he did. Today was no exception. He was asking what was wrong before two minutes had passed.

When Ben resisted, Stefan demanded, "Out with it. What did you do to Carly?"

"Why do you assume I'm at fault?"

"Because you're usually the one who behaves like a horse's ass. Now tell me." Eventually Stefan dragged all the details of this morning's argument out of Ben.

"Good!" he bellowed when Ben told him about giving Carly Angela's name.

"Good? What the h—"

"Now you can stop worrying about your precious hidden identity," Stefan crowed gleefully. "You can get on with more important things. Like hanging on to that woman."

"*That woman* may not want anything to do with me when she reads about Angela and what I did to her."

From Stefan's end of the line there was silence.

"Are you there?" Ben asked after a long moment had passed.

Stefan's voice was low and furious. The familiar tone had been employed often when Ben was intent on self-destruction. "I'm considering whether I should stop wasting my time with you," he said. "How can what happened with Angela have any bearing on Carly?"

"Well, she's pretty damn interested in what happened. Obviously she thinks it's her business."

"Then tell her," Stefan snapped. "Tell her and be done with it. She didn't walk away when you told her about the drugs. This won't ruin anything, either."

"But—"

"Stop hiding," Stefan pleaded. "Don't screw around and lose her. My God, you walked away from the career you wanted because you couldn't live with the past. Don't let it ruin what Carly's given you, too. Please, Ben. Wake up before it's too late." With that, the line went dead.

Too late.

Too damn late.

The words pounded through Ben with disturbing familiarity. Once before he had been too late. When he had stood in the doorway to his own home and watched his wife betray him.

Perhaps Stefan was right this time.

At the very least Ben needed to talk to Carly about what had happened this morning. Maybe in the course of their talking, the truth about Angela would just come out.

With that in mind, he left the restaurant, but he didn't go straight to Carly's. Instead, he sent his boat in the opposite direction. He spent a good hour rehearsing exactly how he would tell her everything. But after he told her, what then? Carly's life was in New York. His was here. Even loving Carly didn't give him the desire to return to the world outside this lake. And Carly had to leave. He couldn't ask her to live within the boundaries he had imposed on himself.

Or could he?

The thought was tantalizing. Ben spent another hour exploring the possibilities.

Misery, as fierce as the heat, weighed Carly down. She had been kicking herself ever since this morning. Why had she lost her patience? Just because her scheduled departure loomed ever closer didn't mean she could start badgering Ben. She at least knew him better than that.

What had happened with his wife had scarred him deeply. She should have respected his wishes and not kept on until he hurled the story at her so angrily. God, the look in his eyes. Whatever their differences had been, he must have loved Angela. He must still love her.

That was a depressing thought.

How did one do battle with a ghost?

Especially if one is in New York.

Groaning, Carly tried not to think about Ben. She had watched his boat leave about midday. Even though she lectured herself about it, she went down to the dock so she'd know the minute he returned. She was going to have to apologize for prying. Even with that decision made, a tiny, nagging voice inside her said that her questions weren't really so out of the ordinary. She was glad when Diana and the boys arrived and claimed all her attention.

Diana had big news. She'd had a date. Announcing it in a breathless voice as soon as her sons were in the water and out of earshot, she stretched her legs out in front of her and smiled. "An honest-to-God date, Carly. Aren't you proud of me?" She didn't pause for Carly's answer. While they unloaded the boat, went to the cabin and returned to the dock, she recounted every minute of the evening she had spent with a man she had met at work. It was such a huge step for her that Carly bore the ceaseless chatter with grace.

"Maybe I'm going to survive, after all," Diana said. "What do you think?"

Carly took her hand and squeezed it. "I never really doubted it."

Yet she had. All summer long, she had worried about her sister, not knowing if Diana was ever going to be able to put the divorce behind her. Since her ex-husband had remarried, she had refused to even discuss him. On those occasions when Carly had called their father in Florida, Diana had been the main topic of conversation. They'd all been worried about her. Countless times Carly had discussed her with Ben.

It occurred to Carly that, aside from Doc and Sam, most of the relationships she and Ben had discussed had been failures. There was her own marriage. Diana's. His own. And beyond that was the tragic triangle involving Ben's mother, his never-seen father and Stefan. It must seem to him that no one made it for forever. No wonder he found discussing his own failure so hard. Carly didn't want to add another chapter to his book.

Making a quick decision, she turned to Diana. "How would you like it if I stayed here?"

Diana's eyes widened. "In the cabin?"

"With Ben."

The blonde sat up a little straighter in her lounge chair and cast a glance toward the house across the cove. "He's asked you?"

"He's going to," Carly said, ignoring the pinprick of doubt.

A brilliant smile spread across Diana's mouth. "Then I say go for it." She let out a little whoop. "Man alive, the Savoy women are making a comeback!"

Immediately she began making plans for all the things Carly and she would do together during the year. Buoyed by that optimism, Carly was giddy with happiness by the time Ben's boat appeared in late afternoon. She greeted him with a smile and a long, promising kiss.

Gray eyes cautious, he held her away from him. "I thought you'd be angry with me."

"I'm the one who made a mistake," she told him. "I'm sorry."

"So am I." He cast an uncertain glance in the direction of Diana and the boys. "Listen, Carly, we need to talk—"

"Yes, we do," she cut in. "I have something important to tell you."

But there was no time for conversation then. J.D. and Griff were demanding Ben's attention. It was Griff's birthday, so there was a special dinner to prepare, a cake to light and presents to unwrap. Ben noticed that Carly's gift bore a card saying it was from them both.

It was a small gesture. Yet it meant so much to him. It made him part of this little charmed circle called a family. After dinner, he sat with Diana and listened like a brother while she talked about her date. Feeling very wise, he patted her hand and told her he was glad she was putting the past aside and getting on with her life. After saying that, he looked up to find Carly in the doorway, watching him with a secret, knowing smile, and he realized the advice he had given Diana might well be applied to his own life and hers.

Later, as Carly laughed and tussled with her two pajama-clad nephews, he thought of how happy she looked, of how much he loved the strong, selfless person she was. This summer had healed her. She could go back and face her old life without fear.

Suddenly he knew that was exactly what she had to do.

If she never went back, then she'd never be sure if she could have handled it. He knew too much about what happened when someone turned their back on the past. He didn't want that for Carly. Much as he wanted her here with him, he didn't want her to have any doubts. She had to go. Then, well, maybe after she had crossed that hurdle they would discuss the future.

He waited to tell her that, but Diana and her sons spent the night and all the next day, leaving Ben and Carly no time to themselves. The next evening, when they were finally alone at his house, he prepared to make the speech he had planned.

But Carly had a speech of her own. With a wide, bright smile, she told Ben she was going to stay at the cove with him.

And all he could say was, "No."

Chapter Ten

Carly wasn't sure she had heard Ben correctly. She waited for him to add something to his cryptic, flat refusal, but he just stood, back toward her, at the railing of his deck. She pushed herself out of her chair and went to his side. "What did you say?"

He drew a deep breath. She looked down and noticed how tightly he gripped the rail. "Ben?"

"I said no," he muttered finally, turning to her. "I don't think you should stay."

A dull ache started in her gut. "You don't want me to?"

"I didn't say that."

"Then why?"

"Because you have to go back."

She put her hand on his arm. "But don't you want me to stay?"

His fingers closed over hers. Briefly. With gathering strength. "That isn't the issue. You have to go back for yourself."

"I'm staying for myself, too."

He turned to her, still holding her hand, his expression as fierce as the clouds that had massed above the mountains. "Carly, please listen to me. You need to go back to your work."

"Someone else can do it. I'm not the only glutton for punishment in the world."

"That isn't the point, either. What you have to do is walk down that same hall where you used to be so afraid."

"I've conquered that."

"Are you sure? Are you certain you can look into everyone's faces and not see the same threats you saw before coming here?"

She started to say yes, but then faltered. "I think so," she said finally. And she lifted her chin. "Anyway, that's not my main concern."

"But maybe it should be."

"Ben, I'm not worried about any stupid, groundless fears anymore."

"Of course you're not. Why should you be afraid here? Remember what you told me? This is the safest place in the world."

"But even here I was afraid in the beginning. Remember?"

His eyes narrowed. His voice roughened. "Yes, I remember. You were like a woman ready to fly apart that first day when I met you."

"I had flown apart." Softly she touched his cheek. "And you put me back together."

He shook his head. "You did that yourself. Maybe I was part of the process, but you were the one who took the first steps. Now you need to see if you can run."

Hurt flooded through Carly. "Why are you pushing me away? I love you, Ben. I want—"

Her next words were lost as he caught her close. "It doesn't have anything to do with love, Carly." He drew a ragged breath.

She threw herself out of his arms. "If you loved me, you'd want me here with you." Her eyes filled with tears, and she felt suddenly very foolish. "I thought you loved me, at least a little. I thought you needed me. But I can see I was wrong."

Ben reached for her. "No, Carly—"

"Please. Just stop." Fighting his touch, she stepped backward.

"No." He caught her before she could flee. Somehow he forced her to look up at him. "Understand me, Carly. I do love you. I do need you."

How she had longed to hear him say that. Yet she hadn't imagined it would be like this, with his expression so full of anguish and her heart so close to breaking. He didn't really love her. But why was he so intent on hurting her? "Let me go." She pushed hard against his chest.

He held her closer. "Not until you understand." She stopped struggling, and his touch gentled. With despair in his voice, he continued, "Carly, you'll regret it the rest of your life if you don't go back."

"You don't know that."

"But I do. I know what it's like to keep running from your past."

"But I'm not you. I'm not afraid—"

"Then go home." His voice was low, hard, not like Ben's voice at all. "Go back to that office where they found you that night."

"No."

"Go back to that room."

The images she thought she had exorcised rose in her mind. *A tap at her door. A long, dark hall.*

She tossed her head to clear them away. "No."

"Walk past that room," Ben muttered. "Then go back and look into it."

There had been the click of a gun. A hand at her throat.

Pushing the memories down, Carly gazed at Ben in horror. Why was he forcing her to do this? Why was he being so cruel? "No, Ben—"

He pressed his face close to hers. "Go back and look into that room, Carly."

She felt the cool glide of the knife on her flesh. The burning in its path.

His hands were like iron bands on her arms. *Other hands had held her this way.* But instead of remembered fear, this time Carly felt only anger.

She struggled against him. "Let me go, Ben. Stop—"

"You have to go back and face it," he insisted.

With a choked sob, Carly launched herself away from him. Back against the deck railing, she screamed, "Stop it!" She put her hand to her mouth to still the trembling of her lips. "You're only trying to frighten me."

"I'm trying to show you why you have to go back. To prove to yourself that you're not afraid anymore."

"I don't need to prove anything. You're using that as an excuse. You want me to leave you alone."

"And you're hiding," he said flatly.

"That's absurd."

"Then prove it." He gestured to the cove. "Leave here and prove you can take it. That's what you set out to do this summer. To regain your strength. If you have, then go test it."

She backed away from him, shaking her head. He could say anything he wanted. He could preach all night long about the reason she needed to leave. But she knew the truth. He just didn't want her here.

He had probably hoped to drive her away with the stories about the drugs. More than likely, he had figured a crusader such as herself would be horrified. But she hadn't been. She had consoled him. She had offered him her body. Time and again. Poor little frightened Carly. Too terrified to be touched. My, but he must have enjoyed overcoming her resistance. It had been what Sam might call a romantic adventure.

Clearly Ben wasn't interested in the long haul. If he loved her, he wouldn't be using the fears she had confessed to him to drive her away.

The anger churned through her, replacing the hurt. "What was I?" she demanded. "Just some kind of summer diversion?"

Ben stepped toward her. "Of course not."

"Stay away from me." She turned to the steps that led to the path. "Just stay away."

"Carly..." He started forward, but Carly eluded him this time.

And like that first night when she had run from his kiss, she flew down the path. Only this time Ben didn't follow. He heard the sputter of the outboard motor. He stood on his deck and watched her cross the cove to her cabin. He thought about all the things he had intended to tell her. It had all gone so wrong. So completely, absolutely wrong.

He needed to go after her. He needed to explain why he was so certain she had to confront her past. He could tell her stories, tales of nights when he had damned himself for not going back to face his own demons. But he was afraid, frightened of what would happen if he faced Carly again. For he was certain he wouldn't have the strength to let her go. If he saw her, all he would do was beg her to stay.

And so he stood, as alone as he'd been when she'd come to the cove. He watched the storm gather over the mountains. He waited until it swept across the lake. Then he let his own tears mingle with the rain.

The roof was leaking.

Jerking awake at the steady *plop plop* of dripping water, Carly sat up and screamed as cold rainwater hit her face. For a minute she expected her father to come barreling out of the door, just as he'd done when the roof had leaked when she was sixteen. She sat, breath held, certain Dad and Margo and Diana and her brother, Sullivan, would materialize from the surrounding gloom. But they didn't.

She was alone.

And the dream of Ben she'd been having was just that. A dream.

Tossing back the sheet she had pulled over herself, she swung her feet out of the hammock. "Nothing like rainwater in the face to bring you back to reality," she grumbled. *Or a lover's deception.*

On that thought, she stumbled across the dim porch, finally reaching the light switch. Then she gazed morosely at the ceiling, where a spreading dark patch gave evidence of the leak she had suspected.

So Ben hadn't repaired the roof, after all. Just as he'd done no more than patch her back together. For if she'd been stronger, more like her old self, surely she wouldn't have blown apart tonight. The old Carly would never have let someone use her as she was so certain Ben had.

But the old Carly didn't exist anymore.

That truth presented itself, cool as the rain-driven breeze that swept across the porch. She shivered. The Carly she had been was forever changed. And all because of one man. Automatically her gaze moved to the house across the cove. Except for the lights that always burned on the dock, all was in darkness. She thought of Ben, sitting alone in the inky blackness, and her heart twisted. She was glad he liked being alone. That was exactly the way she'd leave him. He could stay by himself and perhaps come to regret the excuses he had used to drive her away.

Muttering a curse, she turned on her heel and went inside the cabin. Sleep was an impossibility now. She hadn't expected to doze off when she'd lain down in the hammock. Seething with anger and resentment at Ben, she had meant to pack tonight and leave in the first light of morning. No matter how many times she had traversed the cove in the dark or ridden at night with Ben to the marina across the lake, she didn't feel up to the trip in the murky blackness now.

Her suitcases were open on the bed. Her clothes were jumbled in a heap beside them and on the floor. That's where she'd tossed them when the trembling of her hands had forced her to try to calm down. Now the clock read nearly midnight. She had a great deal to do.

Swiftly, muttering a curse for Ben with every fold she made, Carly finished packing. Then she looked around the cabin. The untidy room gave evidence of the invasion of Diana's boys this weekend. She was tempted to ignore the mess, but the lessons Margo had taught Carly were too well learned. She couldn't leave the place looking this way. Besides, cleaning was the way she had always coped with anxiety.

The porch and main room were set to rights quickly. Followed by the kitchen and bathroom. And still time remained on the clock. Relentlessly Carly climbed the stairs.

She hadn't been up to the room she had shared with Diana since that night she had fallen asleep while reading an old magazine. When Diana and the boys had visited, they had slept on the couches downstairs, in the hammock or in sleeping bags on the porch. The rooms were just as Carly had left them that first week here at the lake. Briefly she remembered planning to paint and buy new curtains. Well, she'd leave that for someone else. But at least she could clear out that closet and toss those old magazines.

She brought some garbage bags up from the kitchen and began stuffing them with magazines. One stack spilled across the floor, several magazines falling open. As she stooped to pick them up, a familiar name caught her eye.

Angela Dane.
Ben's Angela?

Heart slowing, Carly seized the magazine and stared down at the smiling, beautiful face. She didn't remember that face. The caption under the picture said Angela was a rising young star, with a part in a new movie to be released in the spring. A spring nearly seventeen years ago, when Carly had been no more than sixteen. Angela looked little older than that.

Carly didn't remember the movie, couldn't think of anything in which Angela might have appeared. She turned the page, finding one of those statistic sheets fan magazines had been so fond of printing. Angela had been nineteen. She was from a small town in

Florida. The glossy color picture on the facing page showed her to be blond and blue-eyed with a sweet, perfect smile.

She blew one too many lines of coke and then blew her brains out in a Vegas hotel.

Ben's stark words drummed through Carly's head. They were especially startling, considering the angelic face that looked up from the magazine page. What a tragedy. What a waste.

But there was something else Carly remembered. Vaguely. With the same nudging suspicion she had felt the first time she had looked at Ben.

That first day on the roof, she thought, closing her eyes. She saw him clearly. With the sun in his hair. With that cocky smile flashing.

Dropping to her knees, she riffled through the magazines. Had she been sixteen or younger? Frantically she read the dates on the covers. She dug through the pages. Then the picture fell open, and something—anger or shock—roared in Carly's head.

He was younger. The hair was longer. His jaw and upper lip were clean-shaven. But the smile was the same. The eyes, those startlingly gray eyes of his, were unmistakable. The picture was a still from a TV movie. Carly couldn't recall the details or the title, but she remembered this pose, with Ben looking so young and handsome in the sunshine. No doubt she had swooned at the sight of Ben Jamison. Except he wasn't Ben.

His name was B.J. Kyle.

B.J. Ben Jamison.

Dear God, this explained so much. The nagging familiarity. Stefan. The way Ben had talked about the movies they had watched together. Of course he was an insider. Once upon a time he had been what the magazine had so optimistically called Angela. A rising young star.

Only in Ben's case the hype had been true. Carly could remember the television show where he had first appeared. It had been a family drama, one of those topical, intense shows. She had been maybe ten. That put Ben at thirteen or so. He had been the lead character's son. The show had lasted several years. He had grown up in front of America. There had been movies. The covers of many of these magazines.

"Would I have liked you when you were fourteen?"

"Most girls did."

Carly vividly remembered that exchange with Ben. How right he had been. At fourteen he was already a heartthrob for half the nation. And a drug addict, by his own admission.

No, Carly thought. He hadn't been. He had told her that after a first, brief flirtation with drugs, he had found something else that made him high. It had been acting. If memory served her correctly, he had been good at it. He had loved it. She knew that instinctively. Thinking of the night she had watched his jealous eyes devour the television screen, she became even more positive.

She flipped the magazine she held closed and found his young face staring up at her again, from one of those silly cutouts the editors had always placed on the covers. *That first night I met him,* she thought, *if only I had looked all the way through this stack on that first night.* A summer's worth of questions could have been answered just that quickly.

But maybe not.

Knowing that Ben was really B.J. Kyle still didn't explain to her how he had wound up here on Lake Ocoee. Angela, she thought, something to do with Angela. She had made him disappear. And even after she was dead, he had stayed here.

And he'd had the nerve to accuse her of hiding. The excuse he had used to push her away now seemed even more manipulative.

Fury forced Carly to her feet. Clenching the magazine in her fist, she stumbled down the path, to her boat, and across the cove. Dawn was streaking the sky with pink, promising fair weather after last night's storm. It barely registered as she climbed to Ben's house and slammed open the glass door from the deck.

He was coming down the stairs from his loft. Hair tumbled, blue jeans unsnapped, he looked as if he'd been sleeping. Not bothering with preliminaries, Carly threw the magazine at his feet. It landed with the movie still of him faceup.

"How dare you," she said, voice cracking with anger. "How dare *you* accuse *me* of hiding."

Ben knelt slowly and picked up the magazine. *So she knew.* "Where did you get this?"

Her laugh was harsh, just like the lines beneath her weary-looking eyes. "It's been upstairs all summer."

"Upstairs?"

"In my old room," she cried. "Isn't that a kick? To have discovered all your secrets, I should have thrown out those magazines a little sooner."

He looked down at the page again. Was this really him? He didn't spend much time looking in mirrors, but it didn't seem possible that this fresh-faced youngster had grown into the man who stood here feeling so beaten.

"I guess I supplied plenty of laughs for you," Carly said, bringing his gaze back to her. "You and Stefan must have thought it was funny—the way I turned cartwheels trying to figure out who you were. Remember when I said you looked familiar? I was quite a party guest, wasn't I? I must have been entertaining, *B.J.*"

Those final words stung. Ben stepped forward. "That's not my name."

Her voice was husky. "All that fun and I slept with you, too. You've had a nice summer, haven't you?"

"Carly, it's not like—"

"And you expect me to believe anything you say?" Her mouth was a thin, sarcastic twist. "Ben Jamison with his big, sad eyes and his drug problem. Poor Ben. Pitiful Ben. I bet you lied to me about that, too, didn't you?"

"I never lied."

"You only omitted a few facts, right?" Carly spewed out a raw, explicit curse. "Your whole life's a damn lie." She swayed slightly, as if standing was an effort.

Instinctively Ben moved toward her, but she held him off with a dismissing hand. He longed to hold her, to stroke her tangled red-gold hair until she stopped shaking, until she was calm enough to listen to him without judging or interrupting. Somehow he had to make her listen to him.

"I'm not B.J. Kyle," he said again. "B.J. was a name Stefan pinned on me when I got that first part. Before that I was always Ben. Benjamin Jamison Kyle. That's the name my mother put on all my school records. It was part of the story she cooked up for her parents back in Nebraska."

Carly's eyes widened. "Nebraska?"

"Cornfields," Ben said softly, nodding. "That's all she ever told me about the place. God, how she hated cornfields. She was seventeen when she got on a bus."

Disbelievingly Carly shook her head. "It sounds as if you've watched too many old movies."

"Where do you think all the clichés come from?" Ben asked her. "Real life. How many local beauty-pageant winners take off for the bright lights every year?"

"Your mother was one of those?"

Thinking of his mother and all the times he had disappointed her, Ben's voice almost failed him. "She was beautiful," he managed to whisper.

"And your father left her stranded in L.A., right? While Stefan moved into the room next door?"

He nodded. "She wouldn't go home. After she had me, she lied and told her parents she was married and that the man had died in an accident. I don't know whether they really believed her or not, but she kept up the farce for years, until I was about ten and my grandfather died. Then she told me the truth."

"Why?" Carly murmured. "After all those years of lying, why tell you then?"

Ben shrugged. "She wanted me to know the truth." He twisted the magazine in his hands. "I remember the day she told me. I cried for hours." He focused on Carly's drawn features. "You see, in my mind my father was this real great guy. An ordinary Joe. Someone like the father on *Leave It to Beaver*. Stupid, wasn't it?"

Carly's brown-eyed gaze had softened somewhat. She now stood, gripping the back of a chair like a lifeline. "What about Stefan?" she whispered.

"He was always there," Ben said, smiling. "I loved him. And when my mother told me the truth I used to imagine he might be my real father, that there was some deep, dark reason why he couldn't claim me as his. I wanted him to be my father. I wanted someone to put a name or a face to, but she wouldn't even tell me the guy's name—"

"It wasn't Kyle?"

"Hell, no. She made the name up after I was born and she realized she had to think of a story for her parents. On my birth certificate, my father is listed as unknown. My real name's Jamison—Mom's maiden name. I'm surprised some enterprising reporter didn't dig it up."

"So no one knew the truth?"

"Just me and Mom and Stefan." Ben dragged a hand through his hair. "And even Stefan didn't know the man's name. God knows, I begged him for it. I was so angry with my mother for destroying my illusions. I turned into a pretty rotten little kid after that. I fought in school." He clenched his fists. "I took drugs."

"With money you stole?" Carly put in. Again there was a hint of disbelief in her voice.

"Yes," Ben said, trying desperately to make her believe him by just the force of his voice. "That was true. All of that was true. At twelve years old I was headed for major trouble. That's when Mom and Stefan decided to get me involved in acting. Who knew I'd get the second or third part I ever tried for? Then..." He stopped and held up the magazine. "Well, you know the rest."

"Do I?"

She meant his going back to drugs. Feeling profoundly ashamed of all he'd had and thrown away, Ben bowed his head.

"What went wrong?" Carly demanded. "From out here in the hinterlands, we thought you were sitting on top of the world."

The top. Ben wondered if Carly understood what the words meant, the responsibility they carried. Even now he remembered the choking, suffocating feeling of impending failure. It had dogged his heels from the time he was thirteen and someone had noticed that he was a good-looking kid who understood instinctively how to play a part. Perhaps the ability had come from loathing himself so much that he'd preferred being someone, anyone but himself. Much as he liked what he did, he never stopped being afraid it would all end. Maybe the fear was why he had turned to cocaine in the end.

As he remembered the last days, his knees felt weak. Somehow he found himself seated on the bottom step of the stairs. He looked up. Carly was still behind the chair. In the morning sun, which now streamed through the wall of glass, she was pale. The shorts and shirt she had been wearing last night were rumpled here and there and dotted with streaks of something that looked like dust. Her eyes were so cold. Cold, where once they'd been warm.

Why hadn't he told her? Why hadn't he listened to Stefan? Again, Ben glanced down at the magazine picture. Then he threw it aside, wishing it were that easy to toss his past away.

And still she regarded him with those cold eyes. "What went wrong?" she repeated.

He twisted his mouth. What had the reviewers called his expression? A sexy pout? It was about that time he had started reading his own press. He laughed. "Oh, Carly, who can say why a seventeen-year-old gets high? For kicks. For a thrill. To punish his mother for something. All of the above."

"What had she ever done?"

"Nothing. Everything." Ben rubbed his hands across the denim covering his thighs. "The point is I didn't need a reason for what I did. I was flying high. I had all kinds of money. Man, I burned so bright and so fast."

Carly lifted a hand to her mouth. Her eyes glittered with unshed tears. "And what about Angela? How bright did she burn?"

Emotion constricted Ben's throat. He could still see Angela as she had looked the day they met. She was playing a bit part in some easily forgotten television production. He was the star. "She was so sweet," he murmured, only half aware that he spoke the words aloud. "Clean and pure and unspoiled." He looked at Carly. "Like you."

"But you said—"

"The coke?" Ben cut in. "That came later. When Angela and I got married, she was only nineteen, and she'd never done a bad thing in her life. She was beautiful. Ambitious, too. But she had scruples. Values. And I was completely in love with her. For about a year she kept me straight."

The moisture that had been gathering in his eyes now slipped down his cheeks. "And then I sucked her right down with me."

Briefly he covered his face with his hands, brushing the tears impatiently away. Then, making sure he didn't allow his gaze to meet Carly's, he told the rest of the sordid, shameful story.

After that first year of marriage, Angela joined him in the wild life Hollywood offered to those who were young and successful. Cocaine became the drug of choice. They were writing songs about cocaine. Passing it out at parties. Little silver spoons were at the top of everyone's Christmas gift list.

In his infrequent periods of total sobriety, Ben promised Stefan and his mother that he and Angela were cleaning up their act. But they weren't. And despite the fact that he was often unprepared and sloppy in his work, Ben made six films. They couldn't be regarded as classics, but he was thought of as a hot property. In reality he was a sputtering candle, ready to burn out at any moment.

Angela, whose early fanfare had fizzled into secondary roles in low-budget productions, was deeply depressed. Despite his own addiction, Ben could see that she was changing. Her softness faded. She became hard. Bitter. They argued. Took more drugs. They spent a fortune. It was only because Stefan lied to Ben about his earnings that anything at all had been saved. Ben hadn't even bothered to question his income. As long as there was money for coke, he didn't care. He and Angela were slipping into a hazy netherworld where nothing mattered but the next high.

Then Ben's mother died.

The tragedy shocked him straight, but he couldn't manage to stay there on his own. Stefan convinced him to enter a treatment program. Angela kept insisting she didn't have a problem. She stayed in L.A., and when Ben came out of the clinic, determined to help her, she was waiting at home.

In the living room.

Rehearsing a scene with two "producers."

It had been so ugly. So cheap and degrading. Ben's Angel had toppled all the way to earth.

"I walked out," Ben said, finally looking at Carly again. "I turned around and I walked. I left her there. She divorced me." He drew in a deep breath. "And I killed her as surely as if I'd pulled the trigger."

Hand pressed to her mouth, Carly listened as Ben described the years he had spent wandering around the country before settling here. He refused Stefan's every attempt to lure him back to the career he had abandoned. He was afraid that being back in that life would trigger the same weaknesses. He grew a beard. Used his real name. After a while, few people even thought he looked familiar.

"Until me," she whispered.

He nodded.

Silently they faced each other, one on either side of the room, with all that he had told her between them.

Carly couldn't pretend not to be moved by the story. Her initial fear that Ben might be lying had been put aside. She believed him. What's more, she ached for him. For his loneliness. For the guilt and fear that still pulled him down. She loved this man. She couldn't enjoy his misery.

But her anger outweighed everything else she was feeling.

"You should have told me this before now," she whispered.

He spread his hands wide. "How could I?"

"Simple. You open your mouth and you tell the truth." She swallowed the sob that rose inside her. "I told you the truth, Ben. I trusted you enough to do that. Even though it was damn hard, I trusted you."

Pulling himself to his feet, he said, "Don't you understand? How could I tell you—someone who stands for everything that's right—how could I tell you what I'd done to Angela?"

A bubble of fury exploded in front of Carly's eyes. For a moment, she saw nothing but a haze of red. When it cleared, she walked toward Ben. "I loved you. You had to have known that. You're the one who made me love you, made me trust you enough to share the darkest secret of my life. Why couldn't you trust me in the same way?"

"I guess I was afraid," he whispered. "Afraid I'd lose you."

"Didn't you think I was strong enough to take it?"

"I didn't—"

She came to a stop in front of him. "Don't you remember all those things you said about Doc and Sam, about how she accepted his shortcomings, stuck by him? You called it true love, Ben. Didn't you think I was capable of the same? Dear God, I thought we had something special, too. Something true."

He moved forward, too, so that they were inches apart. "Please, Carly. I've hidden these things for so long. It was natural to keep them from you."

"Natural?" Finally the sob she had been fighting broke free. "So you think deceit is the natural way to conduct a relationship?"

"Of course not." Looking shattered, he raked a
hand through his hair. "Try to understand, Carly. I
love you. I never expected to love anyone again, but I
love you. If you had known—"

"We could have avoided a boatload of crap," she
cut in. Tears rained down her face. Ignoring them, she
lifted her hand to Ben's cheek. Silently, with sight and
touch, she memorized the strong planes of his face.
And in the space of a heartbeat she relived every moment of passion and joy and laughter he had given her.
No matter what else had happened, he had brought
her back to life. She couldn't deny that.

She felt his own tears on her fingertips. Drawing her
hand away, she closed that moisture into her fist and
started to walk away.

"No," Ben said, catching her arm. "Stay here,
Carly. I'm sorry. We can work it out. I love you."

At those words, she whipped around. "No, you
don't. If you loved me, you would have trusted me
with the truth."

"We can start again."

"Start again?" Almost hysterical laughter bubbled
up from inside her. "Funny how you want me to stay,
now that it's not my idea anymore. Tell me, Ben, who
taught you to be such a manipulator?"

That stopped him.

Carly slashed out again, eager to hurt him now. "I
don't guess I could expect anything more from you.
Your whole life has been nothing but lies. From your
mother. From your precious Angela—"

"Don't," he muttered, taking her arm again.

She ignored him. "Still defending her?"

"She was my wife," he said roughly. "I let her down. I destroyed her. I destroyed everything."

"And does that mean you have to pay for it the rest of your life? You gave up your career. Your whole life. And that still hasn't brought her back. You can give me up, and that won't bring her back, either."

The dull color that spread across his cheeks told her she'd struck home. That's what it was all about—paying penance for Angela. Because of her, he didn't deserve to be happy again.

"You want to know the biggest joke?" she whispered. "You accused *me* of hiding. You told *me* to face my fears. My God, you even told my sister you were glad she was getting on with her life."

She stepped to the open doorway. "But when are you going to face *your* fears? When are you going to get on with *your* life?" She gazed around the room. The beautiful, empty-of-life room. "If you ever decide to leave your hideaway, you know where to find me."

She didn't look at Ben again before leaving. She didn't want to remember him the way he looked now. In her heart, she was going to carry that picture of him in the sunshine. With his smile wide. His eyes sparkling. Before she'd come into his life and roused all his sleeping demons.

Chapter Eleven

The sun was shining when Ben felt the plane's wheels touch down. He peered out the tiny window. It was just as he remembered it. His stomach lurched, and not because the plane bounced to an unsteady halt near the end of the runway. It was the unsettling amount of late August sunshine. The concrete. And the haze that hung over it all.

Los Angeles.

He kept his face turned very carefully to the window as the suit-and-tie types all around him disregarded the stewardess's instructions to remain in their seats. He was doing his best not to act like someone traveling incognito, but old habits died hard, and it had seemed to him that the man in the aisle seat across the way had looked at him in a strange way several times during the flight from Dallas. Surely no one would recognize him, but there was always that chance.

He needn't have worried. Briefcase tight in hand, the man followed the parade of suits that made for the door the minute the big plane rumbled to its gate.

Ben turned back to the window, deciding to wait until everyone else had deplaned. Ground crews sent trucks and carts scurrying for luggage and food replenishments. God, but everything moved fast. He had forgotten the pace. Time was money.

"Sir?" He looked up. The blond stewardess—the prettiest one—was smiling at him. "You're the last one, sir."

He nodded, grabbed his lone carryon and made for the exit. At the door was another blonde. Her smile was identical to her co-worker's. He had forgotten that, too—the way everyone here began to look the same. "Welcome to California," this stewardess chirped as he passed into the jetway.

Welcome. The word trailed Ben through the big, impersonal airport. It rode beside him in the cab with the silent, unsmiling driver. Yet he didn't begin to feel it until they turned down a broad, familiar street. On each side were sprinkler-fed, manicured lawns. The stuccoed houses were painted in sherbet pastels. They rose from islands of blooming plants and rock sculptures. Quiet. Serene. Private. It looked like the usual Sunday afternoon.

Outside one of those islands, Ben paid the cab-
driver and walked up the drive. With every step he
could hear Carly's voice whispering in his ear.

When are you going to face your *fears? When are
you going to get on with* your *life?*

Heart pounding, he drew strength from her words
as he crossed into the shadowed walkway that led to
the front door. Here, two trees branched overhead,
intertwined with the vines that climbed a trellis wall.
Here, it was cool and fragrant from the mint that grew
in the patch where the morning sun usually touched.
When he was a boy, he had played here, pretending it
was Sherwood Forest and he was Robin Hood and this
was his hideout. Hiding. He had always been hiding—

Put the past behind you.

Again, there was her voice. Ben stopped dawdling
and rang the doorbell.

Stefan answered.

Ben tried and failed to find a greeting.

And for once the dapper, quick-witted man was also
at a loss for words.

At long last, Ben forced a smile. "Since when do
you answer your own door?"

Stefan cleared his throat. The newspaper he held in
one hand crackled. The other hand shook as he lifted
it to remove the reading glasses perched on his nose.
And finally he recovered. His dark eyes flashed, and
his mouth curved into a familiar grin. "And since
when do you ring my doorbell?"

The years fell away as Ben stood there, gazing into his oldest, best friend's face. He felt as if he had flown back in time. Down a long, dark tunnel. Past a hundred mistakes. And at the end there was what there had been since the beginning. All along. No matter what. Just family.

"I decided to come home," Ben said, his voice unsteady.

Stefan nodded, his eyes suspiciously moist and bright as he drew the door open wider. "Welcome back."

And saying to hell with the usual masculine arm-slapping, Ben hugged him.

Shivering, Carly drew her sweater tighter around her shoulders. She eyed the radiator vent beneath the window with disgust. The capricious furnace didn't produce enough heat to keep a nest of mice warm, much less an entire high school during a mid-November cold snap.

She sighed, consoling herself with the fact that this was the first really cold day of the year. They'd been lucky enough to have a warm autumn. She knew from past experience that she'd look back on today with yearning. In the dead of January, when the cold hunkered down over New York for an extended stay, she'd be wearing a down jacket instead of a sweater. Or, if the furnace malfunctioned, everyone in the administrative offices would be in summer clothes.

A knock sounded. She looked up with a smile as the secretary she shared with the other vice-principal peeped around the door. "I'm going now," Maria said.

Carly glanced at the clock on the wall. "I didn't realize it was so late."

"Nearly five." Maria gave her a firm look. "You should go, too."

"Don't worry. I'll be along in a minute."

With a last, warning glance, Maria left, locking the door behind her. Carly sighed, surveying the work still on her desk. But Maria was right. At five, the offices pretty much emptied. Carly never stayed here when everyone was gone.

Dutifully she began gathering file folders and putting them in her briefcase. Her new briefcase. Smiling, she traced her hand over the leather. It was pretty fancy stuff for a poorly paid, stressed-out underling in one of New York's inner-city battle zones.

Diana had sent her the case last week. It had no doubt been purchased at cost from the exclusive leather-and-suede shop she was now managing in Atlanta. The note accompanying the gift had said it was a thank-you for all the encouragement during the past summer.

"Silly of her," Carly murmured now, even as she caressed the cool leather again. Just Sunday evening she had called Diana to scold her for the extravagance and to see how the move was working out.

Diana said the boys liked the new town house and their new school. She had made the decision to move in August, just after her house sold and Carly had left for New York. She said she wanted a new start. Her

ex-husband wasn't entirely thrilled that she was taking the boys out of state, but he hadn't put up too
much of a fight. Maybe he'd decided he'd put Diana
through enough hell already. It all worked out in the
end. His sales territory had recently been changed, and
now he was spending at least one night of every week
in Atlanta with his sons. The boys spent one weekend
a month with him and his new wife. J.D. was still
somewhat resentful, but he was doing as well as could
be expected.

"And what about you?" Carly had asked Diana.
"Like your job?"

Diana had laughed. "Selling expensive leather to
gorgeous executives? Carly, I may have found my
calling. My boss is thinking of opening another store
and putting me in charge of both of them."

"And after only two months on the job." Carly
shook her head. After all of her sister's employment
woes, who would have thought she'd have the chutz-
pah to talk herself into a cushy job. Yet Carly could
imagine Diana, with her easy charm and beautiful
face, doing very well indeed.

"I went to the lake last weekend," Diana said.

Carly pretended indifference. "Oh?"

"Yeah, I brought the boys up to Jim's and decided
to go out and make sure everything was closed up for
the winter."

"Good."

"I didn't see Ben." Diana paused, but when Carly
said nothing, continued, "I stopped in at Doc and

Sam's. They're doing fine, by the way, and said to tell you hello. They told me Ben was out of town.''

"Wonderful."

"Carly, come on—"

"I really don't care where he is," Carly had said, quickly changing the subject by asking about their brother, Sullivan, who had moved from Colorado to Alaska. For once, Diana hadn't pushed.

But now, as Carly sat alone in her darkening, ever-colder office, she wished Diana had given her a little more information. A thousand times since leaving Lake Ocoee, she had reached for the phone, thinking she might call Sam. After all, she hadn't even said goodbye. Very casually, she could probably work Ben into the conversation. She could find out if he was okay, if he missed—

"No." With that single word, Carly started sorting through her desk again. It was time to go home. She didn't need to think about Ben Jamison. She didn't need to worry about him.

But she did.

At odd moments during her busy days, she paused to think about him. If he wasn't at the lake, what was he doing? She didn't like to consider some of the possibilities. No, she refused to believe he had fallen into any of the same traps that had once caught him. If he had, she would never stop blaming herself. She knew that as much as he'd hurt her, she'd wounded him, too.

Maybe if she hadn't been quite so emotional, if she had taken some time to think. Oh well, it was over now. Though it had been tough at first, she knew she could live without Ben Jamison. The summer was long faded.

And she was fine.

More than fine, really. That was one thing Ben had done for her. He had been right to tell her she had to face her fears. Nowadays when she walked down the street or down the hall, she saw only people, not potential monsters looking back at her. She could sit in this office without reliving the horror. She could walk past the supply room, where she had been dragged and left to die, without recoiling in fear.

If she hadn't come back, if she hadn't stared into the face of her darkest terrors, she wondered if she would feel as strong and in control as she did now. Ben had been right. She had proven that the past was behind her.

She only wished Ben could do the same for himself.

Once her anger and hurt had lost their keenest edge, Carly had given some thought to the reasons Ben had hidden himself from the world. She couldn't pretend to know what it was like to be addicted to a drug, to have that craving, that overwhelming desire to escape. Perhaps the only way Ben could fight it was to divorce himself from his old life-style. But Carly thought a person could be an actor without living in the fast lane. Surely he didn't have to give up his craft. Especially since doing so was such a waste of talent.

She had found several of his old movies on videotape. Watching them had been sheer torture, but she had forced herself to do it. The last movie wasn't very good, and knowing what she did about his life at that time, she thought she saw the effects of his addiction. But the talent had been there in the first few films. Even at his worst he had a presence. An intensity. Coiled energy. Unmistakable masculinity. It was the stuff of which screen heroes were made. The reviews she had looked up in the library said he could have been a huge success.

Outside the window a horn blared, and Carly realized she had been daydreaming for much too long. The school was probably empty. She had to go. Even though her fears were conquered, she wasn't foolish. She didn't take unnecessary chances by staying here too late. Closing her briefcase, she started toward the rack where her coat hung.

And there was a soft rap at her door.

Startled, she glanced up. The faint outline of a man could be seen through the frosted glass.

The coppery taste of fear flooded her mouth. Slowly, she began backing toward her desk, hand fumbling for the phone. Then she heard her name, and the fear turned to bright, stinging joy.

Throwing open the door, she walked right into Ben's arms.

It felt like heaven to hold her. As he pressed his face close to her sweet-smelling hair, Ben decided he could die right now and it would be okay. Just the look on her face when she'd seen him was enough to carry him into the ever after.

"How did you get in here?" she said after a moment.

"A kid downstairs let me in."

"But the doors are supposed to be locked. No one gets in after five."

"I guess the kid didn't have a watch. He was going out. I was going in."

Carly groaned against his chest. "And we're supposed to be a secure building." All at once she stiffened in his arms. She looked up, eyes widening. Tentatively she touched a hand to his clean-shaven jaw.

Ben chuckled. "Yeah, it's really me. I had skin under all that hair after all."

Instead of joining him in laughter, Carly stepped out of his embrace, and her eyes, which only a moment ago had been so bright and welcoming, became shuttered. "What are you doing here?"

Ben resisted the urge to pull her back against him. He would much rather be holding her than trying to explain. But he owed her an explanation. "I wanted to tell you that you were right."

"About what?"

"About my hiding."

She clasped her hands in front of her, rubbed them together in the nervous gesture he remembered so well. "And what does that mean?"

He took a step forward, his voice dipping low with emotion. "It means I'm tired. Tired of running from all my memories. Tired of staying away from the two things that mean the most to me." When Carly only looked at him, he cleared his throat. "I'm doing a movie here in New York."

That startled her. She moved back until finally she perched on the edge of her desk. "What kind of movie?"

He shrugged. "It's not much of a part, really. I'm playing a burned-out cop with a drug problem. I guess that's typecasting, but then beggars can't be choosers, can they? At least the movie has the kind of anti-drug message I want to send."

"But when did all this happen?"

"I went back to L.A.," he said. Briefly he told her about those first, unreal days back in fantasyland. Back with the dealmakers and schemers. "Within a week, Stefan had me going on casting calls. Yeah, me, B.J. Kyle, reading for bit parts in TV dramas. Oh, how the mighty are fallen."

Her gaze raked over his face. "But you got a job. And you're okay?"

The muscles in his throat constricted. "Yeah, I got a job. After about a hundred reads, after Stefan called in every favor he was ever owed, I got myself a job, a one-day part on a made-for-cable series. I had two lines, Carly. Two lines." He managed a tight grin.

Carly's heart turned over. What a beating his pride must have taken.

"Anyway," he continued. "I did my two lines, and then I went home, and all I wanted to do was run away. The only place I wanted to be was back at the lake with you. Except that wasn't exactly true. What I really wanted was just you.'' He stepped closer and took her hands in his. ''All I really need is you.''

God, how she loved him. As she looked up into eyes as gray as the November dusk, she realized that no matter what she had told herself or anyone else, she would never be complete without this man. She would never make it without his smile, his passion. She tried to say something, to tell him that, but the words stuck in her throat.

''I want to try it again,'' Ben murmured. ''I want to try everything again.''

Finally she found her voice. ''Everything?''

''Us. Me. The career.''

He caught her hands. ''You told me before that we couldn't start over. But maybe if we started without the deceptions, we could make it work. I'm so sorry I hurt you, Carly. I never set out to do it. This time I'm putting all my cards out on the table.''

Carly stood, and slowly she went back into his arms. She held on tight.

''You can't know how I've missed you,'' Ben whispered. ''After you left, I thought I would die.''

''So did I.''

Hand under her chin, he tipped her face up to his. ''I thought you hated me.''

''I did. But just a little and not for long. How could I hate you when I love you so much?''

Ben let the sweet miracle of her words sink in. Gazing at her glowing, loving face, he wondered why, after all this time, he had finally gotten lucky. By everything he held sacred, he swore he would never take this woman for granted. When all else failed, he would have her. For always, he would have Carly.

He slid his hand through the red-gold glory of her hair. Softly, reverently, he touched her face. In the same way, he kissed her.

The room was full of sounds. Dimly, Carly heard them all. The hiss of the radiator. The click of the second hand on the clock. But the only sound that mattered was the steady beat of her heart pressed so close to the man she loved. That sound was a sweet affirmation of their love.

Drawing away, Ben murmured, "I need you to be with me. Will you be with me, Carly?"

All she could do was nod.

"I'm in New York for a month, at least."

A month, when she wanted a lifetime. "And what then?"

His laughter was rueful. "I'll be damned if I know. Stefan has convinced some unsuspecting person to let me read for a play. It's an established production. If I got the part I could be here for a while."

Joy gripped her. "But that's wonderful."

"Don't get too excited. First I have to get the part."

"You will," she said fiercely. "You can do anything."

His eyes widened as his gaze swept over her face. "When you look at me like that, I really believe it. You make me believe in myself."

"Then I'll always look at you this way."

"And I'll always love you." With a groan, he brought her mouth back to his. And this time the heat spread between them. It spread and grew and warmed. Until there was nothing soft or gentle about the way they kissed. The summer's passion, Carly thought, all over again.

"Marry me," Ben whispered against her lips. Quickly, before she could gather her thoughts, he continued, "If you're worried about your work, we'll find a way to balance everything. I won't take parts in Timbuktu or Outer Mongolia. We'll find a way to work it out. Just say you'll marry me. Say we'll make babies together. Say I'll never be alone again."

What he offered was everything Carly wanted. Ben was right. Somehow, together they'd work everything out. "I'll marry you," she whispered.

Laughing with happiness, he gathered her up, twirled her around the small office. Then, just as suddenly, he was serious. "I need you, you know. Every step of the way, I need you by my side."

"I'll be here."

"It won't be easy."

"I know that."

"I can't promise you it won't get crazy."

"I'm sure it will."

"And when it does I might need to hide from the world in your arms."

Touching his cheek, she smiled up at him. "That's okay. When the road gets a little too rough for both of us, I know a quiet place on a lake in Tennessee where we can always hide away."

His smile was gentle. And so very, very dear. "I might settle for a quiet apartment in New York."

She took his hand and pulled him toward the door. "Then let's go home."

*   *   *   *   *

From *New York Times* Bestselling author
Penny Jordan, a compelling novel of ruthless passion
that will mesmerize readers everywhere!

Penny Jordan

Silver

Real power, true power came from
Rothwell. And Charles vowed to have it,
the earldom and all that went with it.

Silver vowed to destroy Charles, just as surely and
uncaringly as he had destroyed her father; just as he had
intended to destroy her. She needed him to want her . . .
to desire her . . . until he'd do anything to have her.

But first she needed a tutor: a man who wanted no one.
He would help her bait the trap.

**Played out on a glittering international stage,
Silver's story leads her from the luxurious comfort of
British aristocracy into the depths of adventure,
passion and danger.**

AVAILABLE IN OCTOBER!

 HARLEQUIN
®

Take 4 bestselling love stories FREE

Plus get a FREE surprise gift!

PASSPORT TO ROMANCE
SWEEPSTAKES RULES

1. **HOW TO ENTER:** To enter, you must be the age of majority and complete the official entry form, or print your name, address, telephone number and age on a plain piece of paper and mail to: Passport to Romance, P.O. Box 9056, Buffalo, NY 14269-9056. No mechanically reproduced entries accepted.

2. All entries must be received by the CONTEST CLOSING DATE, DECEMBER 31, 1990 TO BE ELIGIBLE.

3. **THE PRIZES:** There will be ten (10) Grand Prizes awarded, each consisting of a choice of a trip for two people from the following list:
   i) London, England (approximate retail value $5,050 U.S.)
   ii) England, Wales and Scotland (approximate retail value $6,400 U.S.)
   iii) Carribean Cruise (approximate retail value $7,300 U.S.)
   iv) Hawaii (approximate retail value $9,550 U.S.)
   v) Greek Island Cruise in the Mediterranean (approximate retail value $12,250 U.S.)
   vi) France (approximate retail value $7,300 U.S.)

4. Any winner may choose to receive any trip or a cash alternative prize of $5,000.00 U.S. in lieu of the trip.

5. **GENERAL RULES:** Odds of winning depend on number of entries received.

6. A random draw will be made by Nielsen Promotion Services, an independent judging organization, on January 29, 1991, in Buffalo, NY. at 11:30 a.m. from all eligible entries received on or before the Contest Closing Date.

7. Any Canadian entrants who are selected must correctly answer a time-limited, mathematical skill-testing question in order to win.

8. Full contest rules may be obtained by sending a stamped, self-addressed envelope to: "Passport to Romance Rules Request", P.O. Box 9998, Saint John, New Brunswick, Canada E2L 4N4.

9. Quebec residents may submit any litigation respecting the conduct and awarding of a prize in this contest to the Régie des loteries et courses du Québec.

10. Payment of taxes other than air and hotel taxes is the sole responsibility of the winner.

11. Void where prohibited by law

COUPON BOOKLET OFFER TERMS

To receive your Free travel-savings coupon booklets, complete the mail-in Offer Certificate on the preceeding page, including the necessary number of proofs-of-purchase, and mail to: Passport to Romance, P.O. Box 9057, Buffalo, NY 14269-9057. The coupon booklets include savings on travel-related products such as car rentals, hotels, cruises, flowers and restaurants. Some restrictions apply. The offer is available in the United States and Canada. Requests must be postmarked by January 25, 1991. Only proofs-of-purchase from specially marked "Passport to Romance" Harlequin® or Silhouette® books will be accepted. The offer certificate must accompany your request and may not be reproduced in any manner. Offer void where prohibited or restricted by law. LIMIT FOUR COUPON BOOKLETS PER NAME, FAMILY, GROUP, ORGANIZATION OR ADDRESS. Please allow up to 8 weeks after receipt of order for shipment. Enter quickly as quantities are limited. Unfulfilled mail-in offer requests will receive free Harlequin® or Silhouette® books (not previously available in retail stores), in quantities equal to the number of proofs-of-purchase required for Levels One to Four, as applicable.

PR-SWPS

OFFICIAL SWEEPSTAKES
ENTRY FORM

Complete and return this Entry Form immediately—the more Entry Forms you submit, the better your chances of winning!
- Entry Forms must be received by **December 31, 1990**
- A random draw will take place on **January 29, 1991**
- Trip must be taken by **December 31, 1991**

3-SSE-1-SW

YES, I want to win a PASSPORT TO ROMANCE vacation for two! I understand the prize includes round-trip air fare, accommodation and a daily spending allowance.

Name_____

Address_____

City_____ State_____ Zip_____

Telephone Number_____ Age_____

Return entries to: **PASSPORT TO ROMANCE**, P.O. Box 9056, Buffalo, NY 14269-9056

© 1990 Harlequin Enterprises Limited

COUPON BOOKLET/OFFER CERTIFICATE

Item	LEVEL ONE Booklet 1	LEVEL TWO Booklet 1 & 2	LEVEL THREE Booklet 1, 2 & 3	LEVEL FOUR Booklet 1, 2, 3 & 4
Booklet 1 = $100+	$100+	$100+	$100+	$100+
Booklet 2 = $200+		$200+	$200+	$200+
Booklet 3 = $300+			$300+	$300+
Booklet 4 = $400+	____	____	____	$400+
Approximate Total Value of Savings	$100+	$300+	$600+	$1,000+
# of Proofs of Purchase Required	4	6	12	18
Check One	____	____	____	____

Name_____

Address_____

City_____ State_____ Zip_____

Return Offer Certificates to **PASSPORT TO ROMANCE** PO Box 9057 Buffalo, NY 14269-9057

Requests must be postmarked by **January 25, 1991**

✂- -

ONE PROOF OF PURCHASE

3-SSE-1

To collect your free coupon booklet you must include the necessary number of proofs-of-purchase with a properly completed Offer Certificate

© 1990 Harlequin Enterprises Limited

See previous page for details